G000240812

Bounty Road

Charles R. Pike

CHELSEA HOUSE
New York, London
1980

Copyright © 1980 by Chelsea House Publishers, a division of
Chelsea House Educational Communications, Inc.
All rights reserved
First published in Great Britain in 1978 by Granada Publishing Limited
Printed and bound in the United States of America
LC: 80-70092
ISBN: 0-87754-241-4

Chelsea House Publishers
Harold Steinberg, Chairman & Publisher
Andrew E. Norman, President
Susan Lusk, Vice President

A Division of Chelsea House Educational Communications, Inc.
133 Christopher Street, New York 10014

Jubal shoved his gun up against her ample breasts, twisting the barrel into her flesh.

"Who's up there?" he snarled. "How many of them?"

She shook her head, and mumbled something that might have been hate or pain or refusal. It didn't matter, because Jimmy Schwatz shouted from the head of the staircase and fired his scattergun. Jubal couldn't hear the words enough to remember them, but he thought the blond outlaw said *"Goddamn you Cade, I knew we shoulda killed you."* After that it all got blocked out behind the roar of the Meteor. . . .

Even Jubal Cade can't fuel his quest for the scarfaced one on vengeance alone. In need of funds, he hires himself out to track down the thieving, bestial thugs of the Dutchman's gang. As bullets fly and blood flows, Cade fights through the freezing, howling Montana winter and the ravages of a death-dealing smallpox epidemic to the bitter end of BOUNTY ROAD.

Also by Charles R. Pike

CHAPTER ONE

Tobe Evans looked up at the sky and slapped his mittened hands together. The damp wool made a soggy clapping sound that got lost in the sudden *whoosh* of snow tumbling clear from a pine-tree. Tobe's breath misted the air around his weather-beaten face and when he sucked a good, deep lungful in, it prickled his throat and chest. He hiked his muffler up over nose and mouth and settled the beaver cap tighter over his grey hair. He hadn't been outside longer than a few minutes, but he could already feel ice crystals forming in his sideburns and moustache.

It was goddam cold and the best remedy for that was whis-key. Tobe slapped his hands some more, stamped his feet a bit, and set off down the street in the direction of Mort's saloon.

Kempton was quiet under the lowering grey-yellow sky. It was like a town holding its breath, waiting for the next on-slaught of winter. And that, Tobe reckoned, wouldn't be long in coming. There was a whole lot more snow up there, just waiting to fall. A man who had lived in the Montana mountains as long as Tobe could taste it in the air. It would be a long, hard winter.

Already the dirt of mainstreet had been churned up by the Fall rains, then frozen into ruts and ankle-twisting runnels by the early frosts. After that had come the first snow. Three days of snow. Then a clear, bright spell that set a mantle of ice over the town. There were icicles hanging like transparent daggers from the eaves of the timber houses, sheening frost over the windows. A pall of pale smoke hung over Kempton, thrown up from every chimney and stove-pipe in the place. The street was empty. Sensible folks were either stoking up on internal warmth in Mort's saloon, or thawing out round their own home-fires.

If Tobe hadn't rowed with his wife he would have been settled comfortably in front of the big stone hearth built into the north side of his cabin. He'd have been roasting his feet up

5

close to the flames and sipping a mug of homebrew. Maybe working on a piece of harness. Mostly just feeling comfortable and warm and safe.

That was about all a man could do when the bad winters set in. And this looked to be a really bad one.

But the argument had happened and Mabel had told him what he could do if he didn't like her cooking. So Tobe had done it and left Mabel to clean up the mess from the west wall and the floor while he went off to Mort's place to get something else to eat and toss a few down with the boys he knew would be clustered round the pine plank bar.

But shit! it was cold.

Tobe was dressed up in his winter regulars. He had a set of longjohns in warm, red flannel under a heavy cotton shirt and broadcloth pants. There was a heavy wool sweater over the shirt and his pants were tucked down inside fur-lined boots of otter pelt, watertight and warm. He wore a check mackinaw with the collar turned up over the muffler so that most of his head was covered by jacket, scarf and cap. And he was still cold. His pistol was belted around his waist under the mackinaw, but the five-pointed star was pinned to the outside of the jacket, just over his heart, so that strangers would know him for the peace officer of Kempton.

He had been sheriff for nine years, ever since the trading post that was now Harry Tyler's drygoods store spawned houses and people came in and set up home. Why anyone should want to bring women and children to the high peaks of the Bitterroots range, Tobe never had rightly understood. It was high mountain country, good for trapping and hunting. Even good for cows if a man could find cattlehands willing to sit out the Winters and fight off Sioux and Blackfeet. But women, no. It wasn't a country for women, except maybe in summer when the flowers blossomed and the high meadows got that lush green colour that seemed to shine out from the hills. Tobe would never have married himself, not unless he found a cushy job and fancied the idea of a cook and housekeeper and bed-warmer. Mabel had filled the bill. Mabel Harknett she had been, then. A widow woman, whose husband got killed trading with the Crow. Tobe had found him up in a stand of lodgepole

6

pine. There were five arrows in his body and his scalp was gone. So were most of his trade goods. The three muskets that fouled his dealings were beside him. Two had burst breech-blocks with blood on the ruptured metal. The third was across his legs. The muzzle was exploded and most of the discharge looked to have gone into Amos's stomach. Tobe had loaded the body on to his packhorse and taken it back to the widow. Mabel had been almost pretty then, and Tobe had taken to her. Even mountainmen settle down sometime. He had courted her for three months. Then they got married by a travelling preacher stranded in Kempton for the Winter. They had three good years before Mabel began to complain. Tobe stayed adamant: he wasn't going anywhere. Not East, or even South to California. He was used to Montana, and at fifty-two, he was making a better living as sheriff than he would working for someone else.

Anyway, he liked Kempton.

There was no particular reason, nor could Tobe have said why if anyone ever bothered to ask him. It was just a feeling, a sense of belonging. A lonely man in a lonely land.

It wasn't much of a town, Kempton. One street that was baked dirt in Summer, mud in the Spring, hard mud in Fall, and ice or deep snow in Winter. There was Mort's saloon, an eating house built off the single-storey cabin that was run by Mort's wife, Tyler's store, a stable, a few other stores and a bank. The bank was open only part of the year. In early Spring Joseph Hodge rode up in a wagon from Missoula and opened up to finance the ranches that were branding calves and getting over the Winter. In the Summer, when the cows were fattening on the lush grass of the high meadows, he went back to civilization. Then, in the Fall, he came back to arrange the finances of the returning drovers, heading back from the cattle markets farther south. This year he had left it late and got caught by the early start of the Winter. The south-bound trails were blocked off by snowfall and swollen creeks; Hodge was waiting an opportune time to leave.

There was a small timber mill cutting pine from the upper slopes, but that was closed down and laid off its hands when the bad snows set in.

In Winter, Kempton was about as close to a ghost town as any place with living people in it can come.

Tobe Evans stepped up from the street on to the swept boardwalk of Mort's saloon. The windows flanking the door were crusted over with ice, and Mort had swung the big wood doors into place across the batwings. Tobe paused in front of them and turned his face down wind. He spat a long, thick stream of tobacco juice on to the snow. It sizzled for a moment, melting a half-inch patch from the edge of an old wagon rut. Somewhere kids were shouting, yelling as they hurled snowballs at one another. Tobe grinned: he liked kids.

He liked whiskey even more, so he dragged the stormdoor back on the left side and went in through the batwings, swinging the heavier wood closed behind him. Inside, the saloon was warm and easy and tempting. Tobe went up to the bar and called for a drink. Mort slid a bottle down and followed it with a fresh-polished glass. He was a good bartender: he didn't ask questions of his customers; just served them and let them do the talking.

Tobe poured a healthy measure and took one first, appreciative sip. That wiped the frost clear of his throat, so he took a second to warm his stomach. That heated him up some, so he took a third to sustain the warmth. Then he swung round and settled his elbows on the bar while he studied the other customers.

Tyler and Hodge were deep in conversation with Jonas Powell, who had a hill ranch some ten miles outside of Kempton. There were five of Powell's hands playing cards down the end of the saloon. Tobe recognized three storekeepers who should have been home with their wives and exchanged smiles. Rosie Dupree was perched on the knee of a cowboy Tobe never had known. She was pulling his ear and whispering words the cowhand was happy to hear. Tobe guessed he came from the Powell spread, and pretty soon would take Rosie to bed. He turned back to his bottle and poured another, confident that all was well. He drank it down and reached for another, thinking what the hell, Mabel can wait.

The comfortable feeling was broken by the roar of blasting

powder and the shrill clatter of ice breaking loose off the frontage.

Tobe ran out into the street, spilling whiskey from his mouth as he fumbled inside his coat, trying to drag the Colt loose.

There was a big black cloud gusting out from the front of Joseph Hodge's bank. There were two men in heavy buffalo coats pointing carbines into the street. There were five horses hitched to the rail fronting the bank.

Tobe fumbled his Peacemaker clear of the mackinaw and started up the street.

It was hard going. The main drag was slippery, iced over. The boardwalks – where they existed – were alternately clean or filled with snow tramped into slush. Walking was difficult.

There was a second explosion. Duller than the first, coming from inside the bank. Then three shots.

Tobe paused. Looked back.

Two cowboys had followed him down the sidewalk; everyone else was hanging back around the entrance to the saloon.

Tobe wet his lips and cocked his Colt. He felt nervous. He had killed three men in pursuit of his duty. Two had been drunken cowhands too fazed by liquor to shoot straight. The third had been a genuine outlaw Tobe had shot down with a Winchester at three hundred paces. The outlaw had been firing a Colt's Dragoon.

Tobe turned back to check his supporters.

The cowboys were still there. Tobe hollered for more support.

Mort came out with his sawed-off in his hands, and three more cowboys followed him. Tyler and Hodge and Powell stayed safe inside the saloon. Tobe checked his forces: five men armed with pistols and one with a scattergun.

He led the way up the street.

Inside the bank Jacob ten Eyck was laughing.

It was the easiest hit he had made in a long career of outlawry. No guards, no clerks, no opposition. Just ride in to this nowhere town and blow the door open. Then blow the front off the safe and take the money.

Easy.

Easy and nice. A tidy cache for the winter, when the stages

stopped running and pickings got hard. Kempton was a gift. Hit fast and run for the hills. Hole up some place and spend the money in the Spring. A sound plan.

Word had come in to Missoula in the late Summer, when Jacob and his gang had been riding out the consequences of hitting the Wyoming stage route. The pickings had been poor and the bulk of the money got spent on horses and ammunition and tying up tongues. They needed a grub-stake to tide them over the Winter months. Kempton offered the prize.

Winter was closing down early; the stage roads were blocked off. That left a whole lot of money waiting up in the hills for someone to take it away. And Jacob ten Eyck saw no reason why he shouldn't be the man to do it.

He had four good old boys with him. His brother, Pieter ten Eyck; Jimmy Schwatz; Hiram Bender; Jeb Greenhaugh. They were all descended from early immigrant families, Dutch or German or Flemish. And they all had one thing in common: a desire to make money. That was mostly denied them back East where European labour was cheap and looked down on. Americans owned the big holdings and exploited anyone who couldn't speak with a Boston accent. So Jacob had gone west and found a new way to make money. A way that let him vent his hate while he took the dollars from the corpses of the Yankee victims of his raids.

Kempton sounded like the ideal place to hit.

After the Fall round-up the town carried close on thirty thousand dollars in notes and coin in the bank. There was one clerk handling the entire transaction. And one lawman, old and creaky, to guard the takings. The snow coming early was a blessing: Jacob took his men up through the hills and waited for the place to get snowed in.

Then he went in.

Pieter blew the door and the safe. Jimmy and Hiram watched the street. Jeb and Pieter and Jacob loaded the money into sacks.

Then the posse showed up.

Jimmy was carrying a single-barrel Meteor with the metal cut down to around eight inches. Hiram Bender had a Colt's Cavalry model in his hand.

Jimmy fired when he saw the posse coming up the street. His first blast killed two cowboys and blinded Tobe Evans in the left eye. Hiram fired three times before Mort's shotgun sent him into cover. Then Jacob and Pieter and Jeb came out from the bank with sacks on their shoulders and the real fight began.

There were four bodies sprawled on the snow. The blood spilling from the wounds melted the crusted rims of the wagon tracks so that the edges got brown and soft and slushed into the runnels.

The outlaws huddled together and set up a concentrated fire down the street.

Tobe Evans got worried.

He watched the cowboys fall dead and then saw the others move back. He thought about letting the raiders go, then decided he had to live up to the promise of his badge. He glanced round. Mort was still with him, so was the ramrod of Powell's spread and one other cowhand.

He moved up the street, twitching his head to clear his vision of the blood filling his left eye.

Something hit him in the chest and he tasted blood in his mouth. He spat it out and levelled his Colt on the group in front of the bank. Three handguns sparked flame. Tobe felt his ribs cave in and fell sideways. He saw one raider go over before his sight clogged up with snow and blood. Then there was only the thunder of the guns and the screams of the wounded. And the tired pain that filled his body up with aching and made it hard for him to breathe.

There were three bullets in Tobe Evans's body. One had shattered his hip on the left side. Another had broken two ribs and punctured the sac of his belly. The third had gone through his right lung. He felt tired and hurt and old. It was lonely on the snow.

He saw Mort go down with most of his face blown away, then a cowboy fall.

Then there was the sound of horses on packed snow, a few more shots. And silence.

After a while Tobe eased his face up clear of the road and tried to stand up. He got partway on to his knees before he fell down and by then Mabel was running wild towards him. He could hear her wailing all the length of the street. He chuckled: it was the first time she'd ever sounded concerned for his welfare, and now it was too late. When she picked him up from the snow and cradled his head in her arms he coughed a long trail of blood over her skirts. Mabel winced. Tobe chuckled. Then he coughed and died.

He was not alone.

Seven cowboys were sprawled across the street. Mort was with them, his shotgun still clutched tight in his hands and five holes in his face and chest. Hiram Bender was down on his knees trying to load a Colt's Frontier model with a broken hand. He was bleeding from his left side and his stomach. There were tears on his face that threatened to freeze over before they reached his chin.

Mabel Evans stood up, letting the corpse of her second husband fall down into the blood that puddled beneath the body. She held Tobe's revolver in both her hands. She walked towards Hiram Bender. She walked slowly because the snow was deep and she wore thin bootees. But she didn't notice the cold numbing her feet. She was conscious only of the cold numbing her soul.

Hiram was still fumbling cartridges into the pistol when he sensed the shadow above him. He looked up. Opened his mouth to scream.

Mabel thrust the big Colt out in front. She held it in both hands, her fingers thin enough to go inside the trigger guard and take up the slack while she hauled the hammer back with both thumbs. She braced her legs wide apart and angled the gun down to point at Hiram's face.

Bender let the scream out.

Mabel let the hammer fall.

Flame blasted from the Colt's muzzle. It flickered out and touched Hiram's lips, cutting off his scream in a thunder of sound. The .45 calibre bullet went in through his parted lips and tore through the back of his neck. It ripped the rear of his mouth away and cut the bones of his upper spine loose from the skull. His head jerked back, dangling limp on the tendons and skin. A fountain of blood burst from his open mouth, spattering crimson over Mabel Evans's dress. Then he slumped sideways and folded over on to the dirty snow.

Mabel dropped the Colt and began to laugh.

She was still laughing when the townsfolk dragged her away and wrapped her in warm blankets and forced whiskey down her throat. Three days later she was still laughing, and people were beginning to wonder if she hadn't lost her mind.

By then Jacob ten Eyck was up in the high mountains with his gang, leading them on to the hideout he had chosen.

It was a settlement built along the valley of a river that cut down through the Bitterroots into Oregon. It was a lonely settlement, cut off by mountains and high-water rivers from anything else around. It was forty miles from Kempton and because it was a religious settlement, there were no guns allowed inside the town.

It was called Hope.

The ten Eyck gang reached Hope six days after hitting Kempton. They were tired and hungry and mean. And Pieter ten Eyck was in the grip of a bad fever.

They rode down through the banked snow towards the sprawl of cabins with Jacob holding his brother upright in the saddle and wiping the snot from his running nose. The younger man was shaking and sweating, near incoherent. Jacob held him straight and sent Jimmy Schwatz and Jeb Greenhaugh in first while he waited with his brother on the outskirts.

Ten minutes later Greenhaugh beckoned them on in. Ten Eyck heeled his horse to a snow-swirling canter that took him past the name-post sticking up from the snow on the eastern edge of the town.

He grinned as he read the name, turning in his saddle to smile at his brother.

'Hope,' he said, 'that's what they call it. They better abandon that, now we've entered.'

CHAPTER TWO

Jubal Cade rode into Kempton with a wild blue norther blasting ice through his bones.

He was wrapped up inside a buffalo coat that kept most of the wind out, but the scarf holding his grey derby on his fresh-cut black hair let too much ice in around his ears and neck. He was shivering and anxious to find somewhere to get a hot meal and a drink before his insides froze.

Kempton didn't look like the place.

It was dark and quiet. The wind played tunes through the icicles decorating the houses, the whistling sound counterpointed by the sharp ringing of steel-shod hooves on steely ice. Halfway down the street Jubal saw a sign that went partway to announcing a stable. Most of it was covered over with snow, but the odd letters still exposed and the outline of the barn, told him it was what he wanted. He turned the grey stallion out of the wind and climbed down from the saddle.

Hammering on the doors brought no response, so he kicked them. There was still no answer from inside. He tried the catch. It was partially frozen, but it lifted when he hammered it with the butt of his Colt. The frame gave in with a tired sigh that sharded ice down from the upper parts of the lintel, and Jubal stepped inside. He eased a crossbar clear of the main doors and kicked them open. Then he led his horse in and closed the doors again.

Most of the stable was empty. There were five horses in the stalls running down both sides of the barn; nine other stalls were strawed and ready and devoid of tenants. He settled the grey inside the nearest stall and pulled the saddle clear of the shivering flanks. Then he rubbed the animal down and spread a blanket over its back. He forked hay into the wall-bucket and filled the water trough from the barrel at the far end of the barn.

When he was sure the horse was settled in, he took the Spencer rifle from the saddle bucket and a well-worn valise from its fastenings on the saddle and went out into the wind.

Outside it was colder than ever. The norther was getting up and testing the land. Snow came down the street in a thick swirl that hid the lights behind a curtain of flickering white. Jubal could feel his coat press tight against his back, and he had to feel down the frontages of the town like a blind man fumbling his way through a white mist that denied vision or sure footing. It brought back memories he preferred to forget* so he concentrated on making his way towards the welcoming light of the saloon.

He could pick that out from the white haze by the warm yellow glow and the creaking, slapping sound of the sign outside. It hung on loops of beaten metal, rusted by rain and slickened by ice. The wind battered against it and buffeted the plank backwards and forwards so that the faded, frosted letters were hard to make out.

The smell and the noise were easy pointers.

Jubal swung the heavy stormdoor open and shouldered the batwings aside.

There was a sudden silence.

He went up to the bar and set the black valise down on the pine table. He set the Spencer alongside; on his side of the bag, where he could reach it fast. Then he unwound the scarf from his hat and face, set the derby down a foot to the left of the rifle and tugged the buttons of his coat open.

The heat of the saloon was thick and heavy after the chilling blast of the wind. Almost as heavy as the stares of the drinkers.

'Whiskey,' he said. 'And food, if you got it.'

'Whiskey I got. Food gets served next door.'

The barkeep pointed at a curtained entrance facing the bar.

'Whiskey first,' grunted Jubal. 'I'm damn' near froze out.'

The bartender reached down and hauled a bottle with no label into sight. He filled Jubal's glass to the brim, then poured a half-measure for himself. Jubal felt the eyes on his back.

'Where you come from?' asked the barkeep. 'Seems kinda late for folks to be travellin'.'

* See Jubal Cade nos. 1-11.

Jubal emptied his glass, shuddering as the raw spirit hit the insides of his belly.

'Come up from Butte,' he said. 'Maybe you can help me.'

'How come?' the barkeep shrugged. 'This place is closed down fer the Winter.'

'I heard tell of a man with a scar across his face.' Jubal traced a line over his forehead. 'Dark haired, and wears two Colts. Good-looking man. Got a laugh that sets women dancing. Mean gunfighter, too.'

The barkeep shook his head.

'Man called Kincaid,' said Jubal. 'Lee Kincaid. I heard he was up around these parts.'

The barman shook his head. 'Sorry, mister, but I never seen nor heard of anyone like that. Last gunfight we had was with the ten Eyck gang. An' I hope that's the last. Christ Jesus! They left eight or nine men dead before they quit.'

'How come?' Jubal asked. 'What's here they might want?'

'Twenty-seven thousand dollars,' grunted the barkeep. 'They took the bank an' lit out fer the north. They killed the sheriff an' a whole lotta other folks. Then they hightailed it off into the mountains. Christ knows where they are now.'

'And there wasn't a man like I described?' said Jubal. 'No one like that with them?'

'Mister,' grunted the bartender, 'I wasn't exactly stickin' my head up to watch the fight. All I know is what I heard about it. An' that was mostly gunfire.'

'Thanks,' said Jubal, 'you're a real help.'

'Perhaps I might be of more help.'

The speaker was a man in his middle years. He wore a grey suit not unlike Jubal's, but with a stripe woven into the cloth. The stripes emphasized the spread of his belly, tucking out where his vest spilled over his belt. There was a span of gold chain running from right to left on his vest, and a swathe of white cloth where the vest failed to meet the waistband of his pants.

'How?' Jubal asked.

'My name is Hodge,' said the man. 'Joseph Hodge. I run the bank up here. The exact sum taken by the outlaws was twenty-seven thousand dollars and forty-nine cents. They killed exactly nine people, amongst them our sheriff, Tobe Evans. I should be happy to put up a reward of at least one thousand dollars for their capture.'

'Dead or alive?' Jubal asked.

Hodge shrugged. 'I want the money returned, that's the important thing.'

Jubal topped his glass and took a slow swallow. The whiskey was poor stuff: homebrew laced with imported liquor, but it warmed the coldness in his belly.

'So why tell me?' he asked.

Hodge smiled and set his own glass down on the bar. 'You said you were looking for a man. Presumably that means you're a bounty hunter. Right now I can use a killer.'

For an instant, Jubal's mouth flattened to a thin line and he felt the stirrings of anger deep inside him. Then he shook his head and sighed gently. Why shouldn't the banker assume he was a bounty hunter? After all, he had spent the past few years chasing Kincaid. Ever since the outlaw killed Jubal's wife. The memory was still painful and he swallowed more whiskey to hide his anguish. 'No,' he said, 'I'm not a bounty hunter. I'm a doctor.'

He pointed at the worn valise.

'But,' Hodge fumbled for the right words, 'you said you were hunting someone.'

Jubal nodded. 'Sure. The man who killed my wife.'

'An outlaw?' Hodge suggested.

Jubal nodded again. 'Yeah. An outlaw. A killer. I heard talk that a feller answering his description was hanging around these parts, so I rode up to check it out.'

'Thieves tend to run together,' said Hodge. 'Like wolves. Maybe this man is with the ten Eyck gang.'

'Could be,' shrugged Jubal, 'but the barkeep says you don't know where the gang went.'

Hodge looked at him, thinking about his next words. There was something strange about this wiry man with the broken front teeth. He didn't look like a bounty man, but he didn't act like a doctor, either. Sure, the grey suit was well-cut, and with the buffalo coat open there was the gleam of a gold watch-chain showing across his vest. The white shirt was surprisingly clean and the black string tie was knotted tidily at the throat. But the waistband of the trousers was hidden under a gunbelt, and the buffalo coat was hiked back to expose the butt of a Colt's Peacemaker. And one hand stayed close to the Spencer even when Cade turned.

Joseph Hodge prided himself on his ability to sum up a man in seconds. It was a valuable asset for a banker, and usually he could reach a decision within moments of talking to a man.

This one was different.

He dressed well. That meant he took care of himself. He bore the outward marks of prosperity: the suit, the clerkish derby, the watch. The valise, for all its battered look, was oiled with saddle soap. The gunbelt, too, looked well-tended, the way a piece of useful equipment appears when the user accepts it as a normal part of his life and takes care of it without thinking much about it. Hodge looked at the face. It was almost youthful, though with a hardness to it, as though dreams had been stamped down and replaced by determination. There was a faint tracery of scar tissue across the bridge of the nose and the front teeth were jagged-edged, as though broken in a fight. The hair was black and cropped close, neatly in keeping with the clothes. The eyes were dark and cold and lonely.

Hodge made a decision.

'You mentioned food,' he said. 'Let me buy you a meal and we can talk some more.'

Jubal grinned. It took years off his face.

'That's fine by me,' he said. 'Let's go.'

Mort's widow laid on deer steaks with fried potatoes and mashed greens. There were hot biscuits and a pot of bitter, black coffee. Afterwards, she opened a can of peaches and served it up with a jug of cream. She liked to see a man eat well, and the stranger looked like he could use a decent meal.

Jubal spoke little while he ate, letting Hodge explain the details of the raid and the need to find the ten Eyck gang. When he was finished ne smiled at the widow and said, 'Thank you, ma'am, that was a fine meal. Best I've eaten in some days.'

Mort's widow smiled back and wondered what such a pleasant young man was doing in Kempton.

Jubal lit a cheroot and drew on the pungent smoke.

'How come you're asking me to find them?' he said. 'There's law in Butte or Missoula, why not go there?'

Hodge shrugged. 'It's not worth their time. Oh, sure, we sent a rider down and the federal marshal came up here. He was here two whole days. Took one look at the snow and went back saying he couldn't follow anyone in this weather.'

'He had a point.' Jubal listened to the wind. 'It'd be hard to track anyone up here.'

Hodge snorted. 'No need to track. There's not more than three places they could've gone.'

'How come you know that?' Jubal asked.

Hodge smiled. Wearily. 'This is a pretty empty country, Cade. There's a few ranches spread through the hills. Nearest is only ten miles out – that's too close. The next four are spaced between thirty and sixty miles. We checked the nearer spreads ourselves. They're clean. The others got too many hands for ten Eyck to risk tangling with. He's not likely to head for Butte or Missoula or Anaconda because he's known there and they got law. That leaves the settlements, like this one.'

'So where are they?' said Jubal. 'You checked them out?'

'No.' Hodge shook his head. 'Closest one is a place called Hope. That's forty miles away over bad country. With this kinda snow coming down, it could take a man four days to get there, and then he wouldn't be welcome.'

Jubal looked curious. Hodge poured more coffee and went on.

'It's a religious settlement. Amish or Quaker, something like that. They don't allow guns in the place and they don't take to strangers. Keep themselves to themselves and no questions asked. Or answered. The others are even farther. Hope lies due north of here, off to the west there's Amity. That's mostly a logging camp. There'd be around a hundred lumberjacks holed up for the Winter, so the odds'd be pretty heavy against ten Eyck. Anyway, Amity's close on sixty miles distant. Then there's Groversville. That's nearer to seventy miles out and it's packed with loggers and trappers. No, my bet's for Hope.'

'So why didn't you take a posse up there?' Jubal asked.

Hodge fanned a hand around his face to clear the smoke of

Jubal's cheroot. 'Too damn' far,' he said. 'And besides, we lost too many men. Hell! Cade, we're not gunfighters, we're peaceable folk. Ten Eyck and his men killed nine people. That generates a powerful amount of fear.'

'So hire yourselves a bounty killer,' grunted Jubal. 'Ship some men in from Butte or Missoula.'

Hodge spread his hands wide. 'Can't be done. There's no one wants to trek through this snow.'

'So why ask me?' Jubal said quietly. 'That is right, isn't it? You are asking me?'

'Yeah, sure I am.' Hodge sounded suddenly tired. 'I'll lay it on the line for you. They took twenty-seven thousand dollars out of my bank. If I don't get that money back, or at least the bodies of ten Eyck and his men, I'm finished. Busted. There won't be a rancher in five hundred miles doesn't hear about it and withdraw his holdings. I can't stand the loss. I *have* to find them.'

Jubal stared at the tip of his cheroot. The cone glowed against the dark wrapping. He reached down to stub it out against a plate. The burning tobacco made a faint sizzling sound.

He had exactly fifty dollars on him. Enough to buy a short-term stake against a long-term Winter. Not enough to leave him free and clear to hunt Kincaid.

'How much?' he asked.

'A thousand,' said Hodge. 'Fifty now, the rest when you bring them in.'

Jubal shook his head. 'No. Half now. The rest when I tell you they're dead.'

Hodge stared hard at his empty cup. 'That's a hard bargain.'

'Mister,' Jubal said slowly, 'you're asking a whole lot of hard work. I don't know why you trust me to do something you can't, but if I agree I'll need that five hundred right now.'

'I'll pay you a hundred,' grunted Hodge.

Jubal wiped his lips on the napkin. He threw the cloth on to the table and pushed his chair back.

'Two hundred,' blurted Hodge.

Jubal stood up. 'You play poker?'

Hodge nodded. 'Sure. Of course I do.'

'Then you know you back a blind draw,' murmured Jubal. 'It just don't look believable otherwise.'

'Christ!' muttered Hodge. 'You drive a hard bargain.'

Jubal shrugged into the buffalo coat. Then he picked up his rifle and the battered black valise and stepped out from the table.

'All right,' said Hodge. 'Five hundred now. The rest later.'

'In notes,' said Jubal. 'And I'll want a written agreement for the rest.'

Hodge nodded. 'I'll see to it now. You better deliver, though. I need those outlaws dead and my money back, otherwise I'm broke.'

Jubal grinned. 'I'll do my best,' he said. 'You can bank on it.'

CHAPTER THREE

Snow swathed Hope under a cold, white blanket.

The ridges towering above the settlement to East and West were great sloping sheets of unbroken white. The pines and aspens flanking the rims were hidden beneath the snow so that even the stark, dark green of the conifers was clouded over and obscured. The light was blinding, the sun reflecting off the glistening crystals strong enough to water eyes and make vision indistinct. Snow covered the low cabins, piled up against doorways and boardwalks. Windows were thick with ice and only those sides holding a stove or fireplace showed wood or stone, and that in patches only.

There were seventeen cabins in Hope. One store, one stable, one empty stockyard. One church. The river ran down the north side, three hundred feet from mainstreet with a bridge crossing over to the five shacks built close against the mountains' edge. The river was the liveliest thing in sight. It ran noisily between narrow, snow-covered banks, tumbling chunks of ice in crazy patterns over its blue-black surface.

A dog barked.

Somewhere up in the hills a wolf answered with a howl. The dog stopped its noise and slunk back to the warmth of its kennel. It curled up and tucked its nose down into the hair of its tail. After a while, it closed its eyes and began to dream about green fields and juicy rabbits.

Silence settled back over Hope.

Charity Lambert shivered and clutched the woollen muffler tighter about her neck. She kept her head down against the wind and concentrated on walking fast because the packed ice struck needles of pain through the soles of her shoes and the woollen socks covering her feet. She blinked a great deal because of the snow-glare and wondered when her father would finish carving the slit-eyed wooden spectacles he promised to make her for the Winter.

To a casual observer, Charity would have looked like a small bundle of cloth and fur struggling its way down the snow-packed street with a wicker-basket clutched tight in its right hand. The basket was covered with a red and white checked cloth, and steam shrouded from the edges. It contained her father's midday meal. Two fat pork chops and a mess of salted potatoes; a thick slab of apple pie and a flask of coffee laced with a dash of apple brandy. Her father was fond of his brandy, maintaining that alcohol taken in small amounts revived the spirits and nurtured the body. In this kind of cold, Charity could only agree with him.

The street was empty. So was her father's store. The windows – real glass shipped up from Butte – were hidden behind the heavy storm-shutters, locked in place with solid wooden pegs. There was no need of locks in Hope. The board-walk fronting the store was chipped clear of ice, as were the steps leading up to it. From the overhanging roof of the porch icicles hung down for a foot or so, broken off where her father had cleared a path for his customers.

Nathan Lambert liked to have things tidy and neat, even in Winter.

Charity went up the steps, slipping a little where the boiling water used to melt the night's frosting had frozen itself. She unlatched the door and stepped inside.

The store was warm, filled up with the heat of the big pot-belly stove at the centre of the floor. Ranged round, and thick-ening the air with a multitude of odours, were her father's goods. There were sides of cured ham dangling from the ceiling hooks, thick strings of heavy sausages and slabs of salted pork along one wall. Along the facing wall was a marble-topped counter with cheeses and pickles and biscuits. A barrel held the last of the Summer's apples, browning now, and close to getting maggoty. The far wall was mostly hidden behind a display of guns and traps and ammunition, the cartons of shells yellowing with age. There was a rack of dresses and a tall stand with poke bonnets hanging from the curved wood hooks; a display counter held ribbon and thread and needles; leather patches and a few hats for men. There were sticks of candy in sugar-crystalled jars and big pots full of salt and pepper. A discreet

23

cupboard contained underwear for both sexes, mostly of rough flannel.

Charity enjoyed the store. It was about the liveliest place in town, and she knew that her father kept a barrel of apple-jack off in the darkest corner for his more favoured customers.

Drinking was mostly frowned on by the elders, like cussing or speaking too loud, or wearing what they called tempting clothing, which seemed to apply to anything not dark and shapeless. But Nathan hung on to his apple-jack and swore that the Good Book favoured the taking of a little wine on suitable occasions.

Charity loved her father and wanted desperately to get away from Hope. She was seventeen years old, and beneath her shapeless coat and severe dress she had the lissom body of a young woman come recently to full femininity. Her eyes were a clear, sparkling hazel in an oval, lightly-tanned face. Her lips were full and of a natural redness. Her waist-length hair was burnished auburn, akin to the colour of an autumn leaf pressed and polished between the pages of a remembrance book.

She set the basket down and pulled off her gloves. Then she unwound the muffler from her neck and face and stepped through to the small room at the rear of the store.

Her father looked up from his stock book and smiled.

'Charity,' he said softly. 'You've brought my meal?'

'Yes, father. Mother says you're to eat it straight away.'

'Aye.' Nathan closed his book and pushed it to one side. 'This weather gives a man an appetite. Will you serve it for me?'

Charity smiled back. 'Of course. Will you eat here, or in the store?'

'The store, I think. It's a mite warmer there.'

Charity went back into the main room. She flipped the cloth from the basket and set a knife and fork and spoon on the counter. Then she produced a tin mug that she filled with coffee, and set out the plates. Her father pulled a high-legged chair up and settled his rangey frame on the hard wood. He picked up the fork and began to eat the potatoes. They were cooked just the way he liked them: salted and with a dash of

24

wild garlic. He ate delicately, savouring each mouthful as though unaccustomed to the succulent taste.

He swallowed and began to cut a chunk of dripping meat from the fattest chop.

Then the door opened and Jacob ten Eyck came in.

Nathan Lambert looked up in surprise. Everyone in town knew he took his meal at this time and avoided disturbing him. To see a stranger enter was a shock, especially at this time of year when casual riders were unheard of. To see a stranger with his beard hung heavy with snow and a Winchester in his hands was a double shock.

To see him followed by three more strangers, all carrying guns and looking mean, made Nathan choke on his food.

He wiped his mouth and stood up.

'Gentlemen.' Nathan was always polite. 'Welcome. What can I do for you?'

Ten Eyck glanced round the store, saw the door at the back, and motioned for Greenhaugh to check the room. Nathan felt a sudden clammy feeling grip his guts. He lost his appetite.

'Who are you?' he said. 'What do you want?'

'It's clear,' called Greenhaugh. 'Ain't nuthin' but some files an' a few crates. No door.'

'What do you want?' Nathan repeated.

Pieter ten Eyck coughed and began to scratch urgently at the underside of his jaw. Jimmy Schwatz eased him down on to a pickle barrel and reached himself a stick of candy from the nearest jar.

'Who are you?' Nathan was conscious of repeating himself, but he couldn't think of anything else to say. 'What do you want?'

Jacob ignored him. 'Jeb, there's cartridges over there. Go get us some. Enough to last a while.'

Greenhaugh began to rummage through the boxes, selecting the necessary calibres.

'You can't do that!' Nathan stepped out from behind the counter. 'You want to buy provisions, you ask me. I'll need to see your money first.'

'See this?' Jacob swung the Winchester up to chest height.

He flipped the lever as he raised the carbine, cocking the hammer. 'This here's our currency.'

The gun levelled on Nathan's throat. The bore looked horribly large. Nathan discovered a piece of gristle lodged in his teeth and wondered if that was the reason his voice sounded squeaky.

'No,' he said. 'You have to pay. Everyone pays.'

Ten Eyck laughed. 'You gonna make us, storekeeper? You gonna call the law in?'

'We don't have a marshal,' mumbled Nathan. 'There's no need. We're a peaceful community.'

'Goddam right,' chuckled Jacob. 'Let's keep it that way. Me an' the boys are real peaceable. When we ain't angered.'

Nathan stared at the muzzle of the Winchester. The big black hole was rock-steady on his throat and he couldn't drag his eyes away. He swallowed a few times, then coughed on the dislodged gristle.

Greenhaugh called from the rear. 'I got .44 and .45, Jacob. The old bastard's got ten-gauge, too.'

'Put 'em in a sack,' replied ten Eyck, 'we can divvy up when we got a place fixed.'

Nathan found his voice again. 'You're staying?' he said.

'Damn' right,' grunted the big outlaw. 'We'll be gracin' yore tidy little town until the snows clear. If you don't like the idea speak up. I'd as soon kill you now as later.'

Nathan licked his lips. He felt very cold despite the sweat trickling down his face and back. A nervous tic started up in his right cheek.

'There's nothing here for you,' he mumbled. 'There's no bank, no stages come through. It's quiet.'

'Just the way we like it right now,' sneered Jacob. 'A nice quiet town with wimmen an' booze an' no one to argue with us.'

'Talkin' of wimmen,' said Jimmy Schwatz, 'reminds me I ain't had one in too long. What's this one look like?'

For the first time since the men had entered the store Charity became aware of the reality of her situation. So far it had been like one of the penny dreadfuls she kept hidden beneath her bed: exciting, possibly violent, but somehow unreal.

26

The facts came home to her with Schwatz's calloused hand.

It grabbed her coat and tore the buttons open in a single movement. Charity gasped and turned away. The coat fell from her shoulders. Greenhaugh laughed and tugged the bonnet from her head, spilling a wild tumble of hair over her shoulders and face.

Charity screamed.

Just once. Then Schwatz slapped her across the mouth.

'Pretty,' he grunted. 'Real pretty.'

He set his scattergun down on the counter and exposed yellow teeth in what passed for a smile. Then he grabbed the front of her dress and ripped it from neck to waist. Greenhaugh seized her from behind, lifting her clear of the floor as Schwatz tugged the dress down over her hips.

Nathan stared in horror. A wild, inarticulate cry burst from his quivering lips as he sprang forwards.

Jacob ten Eyck went on smiling as he squeezed the trigger of the Winchester and blew Nathan Lambert's head loose from his shoulders. The .44 calibre slug ripped in under the store-keeper's jaw. It tore his tongue apart and shattered the bones of his upper spine. Deflected slightly by the impact, the bullet angled to the left and upwards, exiting through the base of Nathan's skull. Nathan's mouth snapped shut hard enough to splinter his teeth. Blood burst from his nostrils and from between his clenched lips. A great chunk of bone and sticky brain matter exploded back from his head and began to drip down the wall behind. His body hit the counter and stood upright for a moment, swaying slightly as though caught in surprise. Then his head tilted forwards and drooped down on to his chest. Crimson covered the white of his shirt front and his legs buckled at the knees. He knelt down, arms dangling beside his body. Then he folded at the waist and pitched over on the floor. One foot drummed for a moment. Blood welled out of the wound in his neck and skull.

Charity screamed.

Jimmy Schwatz laughed and shouted for someone to watch the door as he fumbled with his belt.

Greenhaugh kicked Charity's legs from under her and went

down with her. His unshaven cheeks rasped against her skin as he pressed his mouth to hers and tore at the fastenings of her underclothes.

She bit his tongue, so he banged her head against the planks a few times while Schwatz stripped her.

Then they took her. One by one.

When they were finished Charity curled up in a tight ball, her arms folded against her breasts. There was blood on her face and her hands, more between her legs. It was her first time. She shivered violently, oblivious of the grunting, chuckling men until one dragged her upright and tossed her coat around her shoulders.

'Get yourself dressed, girl,' said Jacob ten Eyck. 'We need someplace to stay an' it might as well be yore cabin. There'll be a spare bed, anyway.'

'Wonder what her ma's like,' leered Greenhaugh. 'Maybe we'll get some more.'

Ten Eyck picked up his carbine. 'Could be, Jeb. We got all Winter to find out.'

They waited until Charity had pulled her ragged clothing back on, then shoved her through the door. Schwatz held her arm and Jacob supported his feverish brother as they stalked up the street towards the Lambert cabin. A few faces showed at half-opened doors, but the wind and the driving snow hid the group and no one came to help. Charity stumbled forwards, conscious only of the pain in her body and her heart. There was another feeling that went alongside the pain, but Charity couldn't clearly understand what it was.

She had never hated anyone before.

They reached her cabin and went inside. Her mother looked up from her chores and gasped at the sight of her daughter and the four men.

Jacob kicked the door shut and grinned.

'I guess it's the season of goodwill,' he said, glancing round the cabin. 'Pity all we got is bad news.'

CHAPTER FOUR

Jubal quit Kempton when the wind died down. The sky was heavy with the threat of fresh snow, but he knew he could wait all Winter for a spell of clear weather. It was better to leave as soon as he could and take his chances on the trail. If there was a trail.

He had spent part of Hodge's advance on a pack horse and provisions. The horse was a heavy-set roan gelding, its coat dense with Winter hair. It was too solid to produce any real turn of speed, but it looked to have the kind of staying power needed for the mountain crossing. The packs contained sufficient food for a two-week journey in addition to oats, ammunition and extra blankets. The saddle horse was rested after three days in the Kempton stable, and eager to be moving again. Jubal had succeeded in replenishing his medical supplies and the old valise was strapped to his saddle on the left side.

Hodge had supplied him with a map of sorts and he followed its directions to the logging road winding up into the mountains north of the town.

The air was still and numbingly cold, but the road was in reasonable condition despite the snow, and he made good time. By noon he was approaching the lumber camp and halted to check the map. The camp was a sprawl of low huts almost invisible under the snow. Off to one side stood the higher frame of a sawmill, even that structure covered with banked snow almost to the second storey. A stream ran east of the mill and Jubal turned that way.

He followed the stream eastwards for a mile or so, then headed due north again. According to the map, Hope lay on a direct line beyond the ridge.

Up on the rim it was colder and the snow got deeper. Whatever trail existed there during the warmer months was gone now, hidden beneath the all-embracing blanket of white. It took him the rest of the afternoon to breast the ridge and get down into the shelter of the trees on the far side. By then it was getting dark and he made camp amongst the pines. He set up a tether-line and rubbed both animals down before spreading blankets over their backs. He doled out some oats and built a fire over which he melted snow in his billycan. Then, confident that the horses were tended, he spread a tarpaulin under the shelter of a low-branched pine and prepared his own meal.

It was very quiet. The sun was hidden behind the western reaches of the Bitterroots, lighting up the low cloud with a fiery red. Soon that faded and the evening got that translucent silvery colour seen only in high mountain country. A thrush warbled one last song before settling down for the night, and a wolf howled, the sound echoing across the snow. The howl was answered and Jubal reached instinctively for the Spencer. He drew the converted carbine from the saddle bucket and checked it over. The protective oil glistened redly in the fire's light and Jubal grinned as he hefted the familiar weight.

The Spencer had been with him a long time. It was outdated by the Winchesters favoured by most Westerners, but for Jubal the old gun held too many memories for him to discard it. Raised in a Chicago orphanage, he had left America to study medicine in England, leaving behind one of the few friends he had known. That friend had died in the bloody fury of the Civil War, but his gun had come back to Jubal. Now the .30 calibre weapon was converted from carbine to rifle, and in Jubal's hands was a deadly piece of machinery. Carefully he slid the gun back inside the sheath and picked up his coffee. His mind wandered back over the years he had carried the rifle. Back to his return to America, an eager young doctor anxious to use his talents tending the sick of the Frontier country. A young doctor with a young wife. Mary.

Mary. He stared into the fire, seeing her face again. Laughing. Loving. Dying.

Dying with Lee Kincaid's bullet in her head.

Since that awful day Jubal had given up his dreams and concentrated solely on two things. One was caring for the blind boy, young Andy Prescott, orphaned by Kincaid. Now Andy, too, was dead and Jubal's life was focussed on the second of his purposes. Finding Kincaid. And killing him.

He became conscious of the mug he was holding and shook his head to clear the melancholy reminiscences. The coffee was cold. He tossed it aside and banked up the fire. Then he huddled down inside his coat and drew a blanket up to his chin.

Soon he was asleep.

The sun woke him and he threw the blanket off. The heavy wool was stiff with frost and when Jubal sat up the cold prickled on his face. He blew the fire to fresh life and set snow to melt while he fed the horses. Then he cooked up some bacon and beans, shaving while the food cooked. When he was done he saddled both animals and kicked snow over the fire and rode on down the ridge.

On the north side the snow was deeper, loose powder that made the horses nervous. It reached up over their knees, almost to their shoulders in places, and Jubal was forced to move slowly, picking his way. The lower parts of the valley were still in shadow and at the bottom he encountered a stream not marked on Hodge's map. It took the better part of a hour before he located a crossing place about three miles west of his route. The stream was dammed up behind a jumble of fallen rock that had trapped a mess of branches and shallowed out the water on the far side. A family of beaver slapped tails in warning as he went over, one big male standing up and baring his teeth as he watched the lone horseman splash through the shallows.

On the north bank the snow got firmer and Jubal steered a diagonal line upwards to the crest. By noon he was over the rim and halted to rest the animals and eat.

That night he found shelter in an enclave of rock that cut off the wind and provided an almost comfortable bed.

In the morning he started off again on the line marked by Hodge. He followed the lee of the ridge along to a split forking down to the next valley bottom and up the far side. The cleft was mostly clear of snow and he made good time, halting when the light faded amongst a stand of ridgepoles.

That night the snow began to fall.

The cold woke Jubal before dawn and he opened his eyes on a white curtain hung down out of a flat, yellow sky. Snow was drifted over his blanket and the horses were standing close together, stamping irritably and flicking their tails against the flakes driving in through the trees. The fire was almost dead and Jubal hurried to stoke it with fresh branches.

Beyond the trees, the terrain was pure white. Visibility was cut down to little more than a few yards and along the wind-break of the conifers, the snow was banked up to waist height. Jubal shivered as he fed the two animals, wondering how long the storm would last. Travel was impossible. The fresh snow would make the going too difficult, and the blinding whiteness would hide pitfalls, let alone the trail itself.

He ate his breakfast and drank two pots of coffee before the blizzard ceased its howling. By then the sun was up, and when the snow quit falling the sky got clear and steely-blue. Jubal checked the gold half-hunter slung across his vest. Like the Spencer, the watch was one more relic of his past. The hands stood at one o'clock. He fought his way through the drifts to check the way ahead. His path lay due north, but the way was blocked by snow that looked too deep to risk. Along the lower slopes he could see the dark shapes of pine and aspen sticking up through the drifts. Judging by the size of the exposed branches he calculated the snow along the bottom to be around ten feet deep. Swearing softly, he got saddled up and led the horses out on a sweeping traverse that followed the line of the upper rim.

By nightfall he was still on the upper slopes, though as the sun went down he thought he saw a likely crossing place. According to the map, he needed to breast the next ridge and then cut back westwards. After that it was a straight climb around the shoulder of the big mountain facing him, then a twisting descent into the valley holding Hope.

If the snow held off he could probably make the settlement in another four days. He wondered if Hodge had lied deliberately about the distance, or if the banker's calculations were based on summertime travelling. Either way there was nothing he could do but wait out the night and push on come morning.

A half mile ahead he could see a long flank of naked rock jutting out from the snow. Trees grew along the overhang, and there were more clustered down the western edge. He headed that way. When he reached the flank he found an area of clear ground, thick with pine needles and sheltered by the trees and the bones of the mountain. The rock face was lit up by the dying sun, its light filtering through the branches to outline the dark mouth of a cave. Jubal grinned as he made for the best shelter he had found so far.

The horses were belly deep in the drifts, moving forwards with a lunging action that cut a swathe through the white. As they reached the edge of the timber the grey halted, its ears flattening back against its skull. Its eyes rolled, exposing the whites, and it let out a shrill, nervous whinny. Jubal drove his heels hard against the flanks, shouting for the animal to go forwards. The drag rope snapped tight along his saddle and he looked back to see the pack horse tugging its head in an attempt to break free. Jubal cursed and slammed his fist down between the stallion's ears. Momentarily stunned, the horse responded to his urging and went on. Once in amongst the pines it began to fight the reins again, its whinnying growing louder.

Jubal slid the Spencer clear of the bucket and swung down from the saddle. Moving fast, he looped the grey's reins tight around a low-hanging branch, then dragged the roan in alongside and lashed the lead rope to the same branch.

Both horses fought to pull free, whickering in fear as they bucked against the tethering lines.

Jubal levered a shell into the breech of the Spencer and looked around. The sun was shining straight down the line of the valley, lighting the clearing with an eerie, crimson glow. There was no sign of danger that Jubal could make out: no tracks, no fire, no sound. But the horses clearly recognized some source of peril and were desperate to escape it. Jubal moved off through the trees, circling slowly towards the rock. The pine needles crunched under his boots, giving off a sweetish odour of resin. He worked his way up to the mouth of the cave.

It was about six feet high at the entrance, a half-circle into which the sun shone bright enough that he could make out the walls and floor for several yards. The rear was in darkness, but he guessed it ran back for twenty feet or more. There was a heavy, musty odour that Jubal didn't recognize. About halfway in there was a litter of white.

Pointing the Spencer into the shadows at the rear, Jubal stepped inside the cave. The musty smell got stronger and when he reached the white objects he recognized them: bones. There were rabbit skulls crushed and broken, the fragmented rib-cage of a deer, tatters of fur. Down one wall he saw scratch marks, as though the stone had been scraped with knives. The marks reached from above his head all the way to the floor.

He checked the rear: it was empty. He eased back outside, scanning the surrounding trees. There was no sign of any movement and he paused for a moment, thinking about his next step. The sun would be gone in a while and there was no better cover offering itself. He decided to chance a meeting with whatever lived inside the cave and began to build a fire. Cradling the rifle in his left arm, he gathered fallen branches, hurrying to get a blaze going before the light went completely.

He got a mess of dried needles and pine cones alight, then built up a stack of heavier pieces. The flames seemed to reassure the horses and he brought them in closer, to where the flickering light threw a circle of brightness over the dark ground.

Still clutching the Spencer, he set about gathering a pile of wood to last him through the night. He was hauling a four-foot length of splintered pine over to the fire when both animals began to scream again.

This time, their cries were full-throated shrieks of pure terror.

Jubal dropped the branch and swung round with the Spencer angling across the clearing. There was still no sign of danger, but suddenly a deep, savage snarl coughed out through the crackling of the fire and the panic-stricken screaming of the horses. Jubal looked up towards the spur of rock.

And saw two scarlet eyes staring at him from fifteen feet above his head.

He swung the Spencer up, squeezing the trigger as the great eyes seemed to lift up and fly down towards him. He powered sideways, pumping the rifle's action as he shifted position. For an instant time seemed frozen. There was a shape, all tawny fur and leering fangs, massive paws outstretched to show talons like curved knife blades. There was a great, rasping, angry roar. The *crack* of the Spencer. Then a blow on his left side that

34

pitched him over on his back with fetid breath gusting warm and nauseating against his face.

Reflex action, rather than coherent thought, swung his arms up in front of his face, thrusting the rifle out like a staff. Teeth snapped shut on the oiled metal of the barrel. Claws tore at his body, ripping chunks of the buffalo coat loose. The forepaws sank into his shoulders, trying to drag him to the mouth.

Jubal braced his arms, fighting to kick the animal clear. In the firelight he could see blood along the left shoulder where his first shot had punctured the hide. He could feel the rear legs pumping at his side as the cougar fought to gut him.

He twisted, ramming the Spencer back against the hind part of the jaw, forcing the mouth open. He turned the rifle, driving the big cat's head over so that it released its grip on his shoulders and batted at the weapon. Jubal pushed out and rolled clear of the great body.

More by luck than judgment he rolled close to the fire. The cougar, wary of the flames, crouched back on powerful hindquarters, snarling as it swiped a paw in a scything arc. Jubal swung the rifle like a club, buying time to get up on his knees. He could hear the two horses screaming and smell the stink of his coat singeing. Then the mountain lion, maddened by hunger and the invasion of its lair, overcame its natural fear of fire and sprang forwards.

Jubal sensed the move from the tensing of the lion's body and made his own play in the same split second. He powered forwards in a low dive that took him under the cougar's leap. He was twisting as he went, jerking the action of the Spencer down and up to settle a load into the firing chamber. The big cat was momentarily confused, turning in mid-air so that it landed awkwardly, giving Jubal time to roll all the way over and come up facing the spitting mouth.

Even so, the cat was faster than any man could hope to be. It was already lurching forwards as Jubal closed the action of the Spencer.

It came up off the ground in a roaring charge that would have landed it on Jubal's belly had he not ducked back. Instead, the man's boots slammed against the cougar's stomach, lifting it up and over. Carried by its own momentum, the cat was hurled over the sprawling body. As the treetops were blocked out by the flying body, Jubal stabbed the rifle straight up and squeezed the trigger.

The bullet tore into the lion's belly, low and to the right. At point-blank range the .30 calibre slug tore through the stomach, exiting high on the right hip. Blood pumped out from the hole and when the cougar landed, it stumbled sideways, its right rear leg useless where the bullet had severed the tendons.

Jubal flipped on to his front. The lion was roaring and snapping at the pain in its side. Jubal's own face was a snarling mask, the killing fury thinning out his lips so that they stretched tight over his gritted teeth. The skin of his face was drawn tight, emphasizing the scar tissue across his nose. His nostrils flared and his eyes blazed. A low grunt, almost akin to the lion's snarl, burst from between his teeth. He levered the Spencer again and thrust the rifle out in front.

The cougar chose that instant to attempt a crabbing, three-legged spring. Its jaws were spread wide. From where Jubal lay they seemed to fill the air, like a massive trap hurtling at his face. He shoved the Spencer out at full stretch, darting the muzzle straight at the lion's face. Instinctively, the cat snapped at the offending metal. The teeth closed on the barrel. Jubal squeezed the trigger.

A jarring shock ran up his right arm and there was a terrific explosion of brilliant yellow flecked through with red.

The lion's skull seemed to act as a sounding drum, magnifying the rifle's detonation as the bullet shattered the great head. The Spencer was torn from Jubal's grip and he rolled sideways, bringing his hands up ready to fight off a fresh attack. None came. Instead, the cougar doubled over, reaching up with its forepaws in a useless attempt to claw the rifle from its mouth. The fangs ground against the barrel and from the rear of the beast's skull four inches of bloodied metal stuck out. It writhed madly, still fighting to drag the Spencer clear. Blood splattered in wide-flown arcs, sizzling as it hit the fire, and the roaring got throatier, choking on metal and death.

Jubal tugged the buffalo coat open and hauled the Colt out. He got up on his feet and stumbled towards the big cat. Yellow eyes that turned to red as they reflected the fire's light glared at him with insensate hatred. He triggered the Colt, levelling the .45 calibre pistol on the heaving chest. The lion coughed and tried to claw him. He fired again. Then again. Blood matted the tawny coat. Jubal emptied the Peacemaker into the massive body.

The cougar growled once, very low and deep. Then it died.

Jubal reloaded the handgun, holding it cocked and ready as he grasped the stock of the Spencer. The rifle came clear with a sticky, grating sound. The foresight snagged on a jagged edge of bone and Jubal tottered back, almost over-balancing.

He was abruptly aware of how weak he felt, and became conscious of pain in his face and hands. When he looked at his hands, he saw long, deep scratchess in his gloves. When he took them off, he saw claw marks on the backs of his hands and a gash across the left palm. His face, too, was cut, along the left side, on the temple and the cheek. He guessed the mountain lion to be a lone male, but innate caution prompted him to clean the bloody rifle and reload before dressing his wounds.

He went over to the far side of the fire and saw that the pack horse was gone. The rope was still lashed to the tree, dangling loose where the crazed gelding had fought hard enough to snap the harness. Jubal cursed and looked out into the darkness. There was no question of looking for the horse until morning. He hoped he could find it.

He quietened the grey stallion and fed it some oats. Then he opened his valise and dug out a bottle of iodine. Using the small silver mirror he habitually carried in his medical kit, he dressed his wounds and covered them as best he could. After that he rummaged through his saddlebags for food. There was a small stock of emergency rations there: some jerky, a little sugar, some salt. He took a mouthful of sugar, letting it melt on his tongue, then chewed slowly on a strip of the dried meat.

After a while he felt steadier on his feet. He had sustained no serious wounds, the buffalo coat protecting him from the lion's clawing, though the coat was ripped all down the left side and part of the front and was letting in the chill night air. The stallion was still restive, scenting the lion's body and the blood. Jubal went over to the corpse and grabbed the hind legs. The

37

cat was around twelve feet from nose to tail, and it weighed heavy. He dragged it over the pine needles, away from the fire. When he got it past the trees he went on hauling until he was a hundred yards out into the snow. The wind was blowing from the north, carrying the smell of the cougar away from the camp. He left it there.

The body looked smaller in death, shrunken in.

'Well, cat,' Jubal murmured as he looked down at the cougar, 'you got nine lives, but I sure whipped you.'

CHAPTER FIVE

The remainder of the night passed quietly.

After Jubal had scuffed needles over the cougar's blood, the grey stallion quieted down and set in to munching its oats. Jubal ate a second strip of jerky and then went to sleep inside the cave. He was too tired to worry about the smell, but he made sure he built up the fire high enough to last through the night. Just in case the cougar had a mate somewhere.

In the morning he saddled up and went looking for the runaway pack horse.

There was a set of tracks going down the mountainside towards the deeper bottom snow. It ran down through stands of timber almost to the floor of the valley. Halfway down Jubal saw secondary tracks cutting in. They criss-crossed the roan's path, then began to converge on the deeper path cut by the horse. After a while they fanned out in a semicircle and the wide swath began to swing in a zig-zag pattern.

Close to the bottom Jubal found what he had been afraid of.

The pack horse was stretched on its side in a patch of bloodstained snow. There were still a few wolves clustered round, ripping at what was left of the roan's carcase. They snarled as Jubal rode closer, but when he fired a couple of shots over their heads, they backed away.

One pack was still intact, though the second was ripped open and the contents strewn out over the snow. Jubal dismounted and looped the grey's reins around the only hitching-place solid enough to hold the stallion. The roan's legs were mostly stripped of meat and the bones were crunched through, but one hind leg remained firm enough to take the big horse's tugging, so Jubal left it there while he checked over his supplies.

He located two boxes of .45 cartridges and three of .30 calibre. There was a bag of salted bacon and seven cans of beans, two of tinned beef and three of pork. His bread had been gnawed, and most of the meat was spoiled. Salt and sugar and coffee were scattered over the snow. He gathered up as much as he could and checked the unopened bag. It contained mostly clothing. He grinned ruefully as he checked through his two clean shirts and his spare underwear. The wind was getting up, so he loaded it all on to the grey and struck out on a rising traverse to the west. The snow was hardened up, making for easier going. He left the dead horse and the remainder of his gear to the wolves. When he got in amongst the trees again, he halted long enough to haul a second layer of flannel underwear over his legs and chest. It went a little way towards combating the growing cold.

He reckoned he had just enough food to see him through to Hope. After that he would need fresh supplies.

If he came out alive.

He rode up towards the path he had picked out the day before. There was a rockslide angling down with a minimum of snow covering the stone. When he reached it, he turned north again and crossed the valley. Then the hard part began. He climbed upwards for the rest of the day, halting when it got dark to build a fire and dole a poor measure of oats from the one sack he had saved from the wolves.

The next day he went on up the mountain.

It took him all of that day to fight his way part of the distance up the steeper slope. The night was cold and lonely, with little shelter. The next night was better: he found a sheltered spot where pines broke up the wind, and afforded wood to make a fire. He reached the crest of the mountain's shoulder the next night.

By then he was above the tree line and passed the night wrapped in the buffalo coat and two blankets under a layer of snow. In the morning he was numb with cold and anxious to move off.

He skirted round the edge of the mountain and found the path Hodge had drawn on the map. By noonday he was back into the trees and glad of the cover. The wind blew fierce and bitter on the high slopes.

He went down on the slant, shifting eastwards along a precipitous trail that threatened to spill over into snow-filled canyons. It turned and twisted, winding down through the trees that seemed to grow thicker as he got lower and farther north. There were streams bisecting the snowfields and beside one he spotted a snowfoot hare and shot it. He spent two hours roasting the animal and eating it. The fresh meat gave him new strength and by nightfall he reckoned he was no more than a half day's ride out of Hope.

That night he checked his guns and filled his pockets with spare shells. He fed the stallion most of the remaining oats and went to sleep looking forward to seeing people again.

Even the ten Eyck gang.

In the morning he shaved and doled out the last of the horse's feed. He treated himself to extra rations, too.

Then he mounted up and went on down the mountain.

Hodge had been vague about the exact location of Hope. The banker had never seen the settlement himself and only a few of Kempton's citizens had talked with Hopers coming in for supplies. As best they knew, the place was built beside a river that ran around the foot of the mountain Jubal had just crossed. Exactly where along the river it lay, they were unsure.

Jubal halted at noon and let the grey rest while he scanned the land below.

It was slightly warmer here, as though the Bitterroots protected this section from the wind. Timber grew in heavy stands all the way down to the bottom, untouched. Directly below Jubal's position was a wide plateau, a kind of massive ledge jutting out from the steeper slope. In Summer, he guessed, it would be rich with grass. After eating, he went on down.

From the plateau he got a better view of the valley. On the north side, the mountains rose up in a massive chain that was hidden behind cloud at the top. The rocks curved round to the east, sheltering the valley from wind and a good deal of snowfall. Westwards wound a narrow pass, hooking away into the distance with a fast-flowing river running black along its bottom. There was an area of cleared ground along one of the lower slopes, as though timber had been cut and shipped out.

For want of any other target to aim for, Jubal headed that way.

It took him all afternoon to work his way down, but when he got to the river he saw Hope.

From the upper reaches of the mountains, the settlement was hidden behind a series of high meadows. They ran down like gigantic terraces to the ground below, combining with the curvature of the hills to cradle Hope in a bowl of rock that simultaneously sheltered and camouflaged the little town.

The snow was packed hard along the river, shining bright in the cold Winter sun. It made a decent enough trail and before twilight he was in sight of Hope.

All along he had been uncertain of the town's exact nature, not sure what to expect of a religious settlement that chose to hide itself so far from any other human life. What he saw still managed to surprise him.

Hope was tiny.

He counted the cabins from the shelter of a pine break and estimated that there couldn't be more than thirty or so able-bodied men living there. And that was assuming that each cabin held a grown man with a grown son. Allow one man and his wife for each cabin. Add a son: thirty-four men. Assume some of the older folk were too aged to be useful in a fight, and that some of the children were too young to carry a gun. Remember that Hodge had told him the Hopers didn't use guns.

The odds built up in favour of the ten Eyck gang.

Built up awful high.

Hodge had said that four outlaws got away from Kempton. Four men with guns. Men who knew how to use them.

Riding in blind would be like trying to fill a straight flush on a blind card.

Jubal began to wonder if he had made a mistake.

Then the thought of Hodge's second five hundred dollars and the possibility of finding Kincaid overcame the doubts. Anyway, he told himself, he needed food. And he had come too far to go back.

Jubal looked up at the sky. The sun was going down fast, shadowing the valley. Four men – even with guns – would have problems holding a whole town down. If he waited until night he should be able to go in unseen.

Maybe.

He reached inside his tattered coat, fumbling through the frosted hide to the inner pocket of his jacket. He pulled a

42

cheroot loose and stuck it in his mouth. Then he struck a match against his saddlehorn and lit the slender tube of dark tobacco.

The smoke filled his lungs and curled out from his lips and nose. He sat watching the settlement as he smoked, thinking.

All right. Jacob ten Eyck was the Ace heading the hand. Hodge had said the outlaw always rode with his brother, Pieter. Let Pieter, then, be the King. Two more men. The Queen and the Ten.

With Jubal playing the Jack. The blind card.

He tossed his cheroot stub into the snow as the sun faded away behind the hills.

'Let's go,' he grunted. 'We'll fill the straight or get flushed out.'

CHAPTER SIX

Charity stumbled towards the cabin, almost falling as the heavy bucket threatened to drag her forwards and pitch her over on the ice.

She bit her lower lip as she fought to keep her balance. Water slopped over her felt boots, but she ignored that. Her blood was warm and salty on the inside of her mouth and it filled her mind with wild ideas.

Hating someone was wrong.

Wanting to see a man's body stretched out on the snow with hot, sticky blood pumping from bullet holes was wrong.

Hoping someone would die was wrong.

Her father had taught her that.

But her father was dead.

His blood was salty. Warm, too.

She had tasted it back in the store when she turned her head away from the stubbly lips of the rapists and saw the pool welling out from under her father's face.

She had forgotten the sensation then because there were too many other sensations pressing into her body.

Pain, first. Then the hot wetness between her legs. Then more pain.

The numbing ache where her skull was bounced against the bare planks.

The rasp of a beard against her lips and cheeks.

The other pain that started where the wetness began and climbed up through her stomach into her nerves so that her fingers clenched tight and drove her nails into her palms.

After that, the dull, continuing ache that seemed to fill her body and crawl inside her mind until all she could feel was its drumming against the walls of her skull and the walls of her soul.

They had raped her twice more, then forgotten her as they sought fresh victims. Victims more lively than Charity.

Her eyes were dull, the sparkle gone. Her hair hung lank and untended. Her clothes were dirty, unchanged since the first time when she tore them off and tried to bathe the hurt away.

They had come back then and found her crouched in the hip bath. Dragged her out and taken her again on the warm floor. When her mother screamed and fought them, they took her, too. Then shot her when she ripped livid gouges down the man called Jeb's face.

Charity had laughed at the blood.

So they turned back and spent their anger in her body.

That had been – what? – ten days ago? Twelve? She wasn't sure. She wasn't sure of anything now.

Except one thing.

She wanted to see them die. It didn't matter what her father had told her. A man might turn his cheek and accept the second blow without argument, but it was different for a woman. The blows didn't land on the cheek. They went inside. In to that place of secrecy that was held in trust for the right man; the one man. The only man.

Now she was spoiled.

Now she bore their taint.

She was stained and cursed. A harlot. A woman despised. She felt dirty, sullied.

She hoped they would be killed when they went away. She hoped that a posse would be waiting to shoot them down. She hoped they might die slowly. In pieces, bit by bit; as she was.

The youngest one was dying already.

Charity could sense that from his fever and the ugly swelling of his glands that thrust hard lumps up from his neck and armpits and groin.

She had never seen a naked man before, not even her dead father, but the outlaws forced her to tend their sick companion. Pieter was his name, and she was made to bathe him. They had killed her mother and dragged the body out to the river. Tossed it in, denying Verity Lambert even the decency of a Christian burial. Then they took over the cabin and the town.

They had gone out into the street and fired their guns until everyone came out to see what was happening. Then they had told the people they would be staying through the Winter and

45

would need food and drink and women. And that they would kill anyone who argued.

Jonathan Hardy, who was the oldest inhabitant and led the prayers in church, had stepped forward and told them to leave.

They had shot him down in the street.

His two sons, Jacob and Jonas, ran forwards. And died.

Matthew Galant had shouted that they were only four men and the Hopers could disarm them and drive them away.

Matthew had gone down in his own blood with his face ravaged by the shotgun the little blond man called Jimmy carried.

Luke Garfield and James Smith, John Parker and Jebediah Cole, Caleb Hunter, even little Aaron Baldry, had died.

Old Granny Galant and Martha Parker and Mary Cole were shot dead, too.

The others cowered back and stared at the bodies. They covered the snow with blood. Charity could hardly believe that human beings carried so much blood inside them. It spilled out and spread over the snow. It ran down inside the runnels of the wagon tracks and even melted the edges of the hard lines. Hope filled up with a bitter pall of black smoke. It hung like a funeral cloth across the street. It stung eyes and set people to coughing through their tears.

When the guns stopped firing the settlement was weirdly quiet.

Then the outlaws had repeated their demands and picked out the best-looking girls from amongst the terrified onlookers.

They took Rachel Garfield, who was only twenty years old and fair as the Summer corn; the daughter of Jared Kleinman, who was dark as Rachel was fair; Sarah Harton, younger even that Charity.

Susan Kleinman was found the next morning with a rope around her neck, her feet well clear of the stoop she had chosen to hang herself from.

They went back and took Norah Lofts.

They said they were saving Charity for when Pieter got well again.

That was why Charity decided against following Susan's example and killing herself: she wanted to see Pieter die.

She felt reasonably confident that it wouldn't be long. He

was badly fevered, and the swellings on his body got bigger and harder every day. He complained all the time of pains in his joints, and most of the food she gave him was thrown back, as though his belly was too disturbed to accept honest meat. Charity prepared his meals separately to the others. She succeeded in convincing Jacob ten Eyck that his brother needed a special diet. Then she added extra salt and far too much pepper, which increased the fever. There were herbs stored in the outhouse, most of them medicinal, some used as purgatives. She took to adding these, too, so that the young outlaw's stomach was slowly poisoned even more than by his sickness.

It was the only way she could think of to revenge her parents. She hoped she would be forgiven when the time came.

After the first few days the outlaws had decided to quit the Lambert cabin and take up residence in separate homes. They had driven parents and children out to find shelter where they could, and settled in with their chosen women.

No one dared argue, and Charity was glad. The move left her free to feed Pieter whatever she fancied. So far she had tried about half the stock of herbs and he was getting sicker each day.

The others came to visit when they thought about it. Jacob ten Eyck came twice, sometimes three times, a day. Jeb Greenhaugh and Jimmy Schwatz – by now their names were printed on Charity's mind – showed up just often enough to persuade Jacob they really cared. They stayed outside the cabin, calling in through the windows even though Pieter could no longer understand what they shouted. They were obviously frightened of catching whatever it was Pieter had.

Charity wasn't. She hoped she had the disease already.

So that she could pass it on to the others.

She sniffed noisily and set the bucket down. Maybe she was getting it. Her nose had been running a lot recently, and her arms ached more than usual. She wiped a mitten across her nose and reached down for the bucket.

Then a shadow blocked out the dim light of the window and a man swung the galvanized tin out of her reach.

'Let me do that, ma'am,' murmured Jubal Cade. 'It looks kind of heavy.'

Charity jumped back, one hand lifting automatically to cover her face.

'It's all right, ma'am. I don't mean you no harm. Just thought I'd help you a bit.'

'Who are you?'

For no reason she could define, Charity kept her own voice down to a low whisper.

'Name's Cade, ma'am. Jubal Cade. I'm a doctor.'

It was the kind of meaningless phrase that generally reassured people, even though anyone could say it. Mostly it worked. In this case, not.

'Why you carrying a rifle, then?' Charity's voice lifted up towards a normal level. Then it got higher 'You're one of them!'

'No.' Jubal swung the bucket away and down. 'I came up here to help you. I came to get the ten Eyck gang.'

Charity laughed. In the lonely night her tittering held the sound of madness.

'Why?'

'Several reasons,' grunted Jubal. 'The folks in Kempton want the gang brought in. I got reasons of my own.'

'So do I.' Her voice was no longer that of an innocent girl. 'Dear Lord, so do I.'

'Then maybe we can work together,' said Jubal, deliberately modulating his tone. 'Want to talk about it?'

Charity shook her head. 'No. Jacob'll be coming over to see his brother any time now. If I'm not there, he'll come looking. Then he'll hurt me. That'd be your fault, Mister Cade.'

'I came to help you,' Jubal repeated. 'Don't you trust me?'

'No,' said the girl, her voice suddenly even again. 'I don't trust any man no more.'

'I'm a doctor,' Jubal repeated. 'You can trust me.'

'Why?' She began to shake her head. 'Why should I?'

'Why should I come up here?' Jubal was thinking fast, choosing his words carefully so as to assure the girl of his intentions. 'If I was with the gang I'd have ridden straight in. You understand? I'd've gone straight to them. I didn't. I came to you because I need your help. I need somewhere to stable my horse and I need food. I came to help you.'

'Oh, sweet Jesus,' gasped Charity. And threw herself against him. 'You came to help me.'

'Sure.' Jubal settled his left arm around her shoulders. He kept the right free: it held the Spencer. 'Of course I did.'

'You'll kill them?' Her voice was a harsh whisper now. 'You will kill them, won't you?'

'If I must.' He could feel her trembling through all the layers of both their clothing. 'But I'll need help. You'll have to tell me where they are and how many.'

'Yes. Dear God, yes.' Charity began to cry. It was the first time since the pain started. 'I will. I promise I will.'

She pulled away, fumbling at her eyes with grubby mittens.

'Wait here. I have to go bathe Pieter. He's sick, you know. I think he's dying, but I better be there when Jacob comes. I'll slip out afterwards. No one watches me any more.' Her voice got pitched high again. 'They don't care about me any more. Not now.'

She picked up the bucket and started back in the direction of the cabin. Jubal watched her go, not sure whether he should trust her or stop her. He had seen cases of hysteria before, and a few of madness. This girl seemed poised between the two. There was no way to tell if she would betray him or help him; on balance, it seemed a better bet to opt for the latter choice.

Maybe the girl was the Jack that would fill the hand.

He drifted back to the river and fetched the grey stallion up halfway to the cabin.

The sky was clouding over, heavy stormheads blotting out the moon so that the only light came from the cabins spread along Hope's single street. There were only four or five lit, but from one of them came the sound of laughter and music, the scraping of a fiddle and the off-key wailing of an accordion accompanied by an equally untuned voice.

Jubal waited.

It was an hour before the girl got back. When she came she was carrying a small pot that spread a cloud of steam around her.

'I brought you some stew, Mister Cade. I thought you'd be getting hungry.'

'Thanks,' said Jubal, 'I appreciate that.'

So far his gamble was paying off.

The stew tasted good and he ate it hungrily. It took him only a few minutes. The girl waited while he spooned the meat and vegetables into his mouth, then held her hands out for the pot. Jubal passed it back and smiled at her.

'You cook a fine meal, miss.'

'Charity Lambert.' Her voice was even again, almost conversational. 'I'm the daughter of Nathan and Verity Lambert. They killed my parents.'

'They've killed a lot of people,' said Jubal, 'that's why I'm here. I'd like you to tell me about them, but I'd like to get my horse under cover first.'

Charity nodded. 'There's a stable down the road a bit. They keep their horses in there, but they don't go there much. They leave that to the men. There's a shed at the back they never go into, you could hide your horse in there.'

'Fine,' said Jubal. 'You want to show me the way?'

She nodded and set off through the snow covering the open ground between the cabins and the river. Across the water Jubal could pick out the remnants of several cabins that looked to be burned out. When he asked Charity about them she shook her head and pulled a face.

'They burned the places that side. Said they were too far away. The families living there have all moved into town.'

'How about the bridge?' Jubal asked. 'They burn that, too?'

'No. It doesn't go anywhere, except to the cabins and the trees we cut for timber.'

Jubal recalled the open space he had seen coming in. 'The logging road?'

The girl nodded. 'Yes, that's right.'

'And it doesn't go anywhere? There's no trail over the mountains?'

'No. We never thought to need one. There's only one way in to Hope. I suppose you must have come that way, down from the south.'

Jubal nodded in turn. 'Yeah, that was the way.'

They reached the stable and the girl went on ahead. After a while she came back and beckoned him on. The stable was a low-roofed barn with .. snowed-over corral behind. Alongside the corral was a dilapidated shed only just big enough to accommodate the grey stallion. Charity led the way in and left Jubal to unsaddle while she fetched oats and straw from the main building. When they got the horse bedded down they closed the door and propped it shut with broken timbers from the fencing of the corral. The way the sky was shaping up, all signs of their entry would be hidden by morning.

'Now you'll need somewhere to hide,' said Charity. 'Our ... my cabin should be safe.'

'How's that?' Jubal asked. 'You said you had one of the gang in there with you.'

Charity laughed. 'He won't know you're there. He's too sick. Remember? I told you he was sick. He's been feverish since he got here. He's been getting worse all the time.'

'So who tends him?' Jubal said. 'You do it on your own?'

She nodded. 'His brother visits every day. Three or four times. The others come, too, but they stay outside. They're afraid of catching it. There's no one else. Only Jacob and me go close to him.' She chuckled, the tinge of insanity coming back into her voice. 'He's dying, is Pieter. They're all afraid. Besides, we got a big cabin, there's three rooms now momma and poppa are gone. You can stay in with me. I trust you. And no one ever comes in there.'

'All right,' grunted Jubal, 'show me the way.'

They went back through the snow and came up to the cabin from behind. There was a single light burning in a window off to the left side. To the right, beyond a narrow door, was a second, dark, window. Charity motioned for him to wait and opened the door. A few minutes later she reappeared and beckoned him in.

The cabin was clean and compact. A door opened off the rear into the lit room, and Jubal could hear the faint sounds of fretful sleep. Facing that room was another door, swung partway open. Charity ushered him in, stepping across the narrow corridor to listen for a moment at Pieter's door. She appeared satisfied that the sick outlaw was unconscious, or too weak to present any threat and went on into the main room. Jubal followed.

It was a large room for a cabin, seeming more spacious

51

thanks to the starkness of the furnishings. The floor was scrubbed pine with a ragged woollen carpet set in front of an open hearth. There was a cooking range built off to one side, a pine table and four rough chairs that looked functional rather than comfortable. A well-patched settee was the only concession to luxury and the most ornate piece of furniture was a curlicued bookcase with glass doors covering the volumes inside. Jubal glanced at the titles: the books were almost exclusively religious tracts or farming manuals. There was a seed catalogue and a tract on livestock. Pots and pans were ranged neatly on shelves beside the range, and Jubal guessed that the cupboard on the other side contained food.

The room had an air of austere simplicity, of emptiness. It hardly felt like a place where people lived.

The windows facing on to the street were shuttered, plain gingham curtains drawn across the thick wood. Charity slipped the latch down on the door and hurried back to the bedroom.

Like the main quarters, this was stark and simple. A narrow bunk, a chair, and a plain wardrobe comprised the only furniture. The floor was bare and there were none of the frills normally associated with a young woman's room.

'Wait here,' Charity whispered. 'I'll make some coffee.'

Jubal murmured his thanks. He was beginning to feel the effects of the long ride and the hours without sleep. He sat down on the bed and tossed his derby on the chair. Slowly, keeping the Spencer close at hand, he unwound the scarf from his neck and shucked out of the buffalo coat. There was a peg set into the rear of the door so he hung his outer clothing there and checked the narrow window. It, too, was shuttered, the wood held in place by a metal hook fastening into an eye. It occurred to him that the whole cabin was surprisingly vulnerable. There were none of the customary defences of a frontier cabin.

Maybe that was due to some religious conviction. He wasn't sure, nor did he care too much. The mattress on the bed was soft, covered with a checkered quilt. He eased back, resting his head against the wall, and waited for the girl to return.

She came back with two steaming mugs and settled herself wearily on the chair.

'Pieter's asleep now,' she said softly. 'We can talk so long as we keep our voices down. No one will come around now.'

Jubal sipped his coffee and thought about his next move. Before he tried anything he needed to be sure of several facts.

'How many are there in the gang?' he asked.

'Four,' was the reply. 'There's Pieter and his brother, Jacob. Then a man called Jeb Greenhaugh and another called Jimmy Schwatz.'

'Not one called Kincaid? Tall man with a scar across his forehead?'

She shook her head. 'No, just the four of them.'

'Where are the others? They stay together, or they in separate cabins?'

'They've taken a cabin apiece,' sighed Charity. 'They chose a woman each, and then turned people out of whichever place they fancied.'

'How long's Pieter been sick?'

'He was feverish when he got here.' Charity's eyes blazed at the thought. 'He's been getting worse ever since. Mostly, he's delirious. He's dying, you know.'

'I'll take a look at him in a bit,' said Jubal, 'but let's talk some more first. How many menfolk are there?'

'Nine,' she answered. 'They killed the others.'

'You got any weapons?'

Charity frowned. 'Guns, you mean? We don't believe in firearms, Mister Cade.'

'But you must have some weapons,' Jubal insisted. 'Don't you folks hunt? What about Indians?'

Charity smiled. It was a sour expression. 'We had two rifles and a few shotguns, but they took all of them. They're locked up in Jacob ten Eyck's cabin. We only used them for hunting because the Indians never harmed us. The Sioux don't come this far west and the Nez Perce leave us be. We don't believe in violence.'

'Sometimes,' murmured Jubal bitterly, 'it's the only way.'

'I think you may well be right.' Charity's tone was flat, disillusioned. 'Poppa kept guns in his store. He sold them to trappers. The Elders didn't approve, but it brought us money for seeds and cattle, so they let it go on.'

'They still there?' asked Jubal. 'In the store?'

She nodded. 'Yes, but the store's locked up. Jacob has the key.'

'Suppose I got the store open.' Jubal noticed she was scratching at her wrists. 'Would your people use the guns?'

Charity thought for a moment, then shook her head.

'No, it's against our religion. "Thou shalt not kill". We hold to that.'

'The Bible also says to take an eye for an eye,' Jubal countered. 'And surely folks have a right to defend themselves?'

'I'd help you.' That tinge of madness he had heard earlier crept back into Charity's voice. 'I'd use a gun because of what they did.'

Jubal could guess what that had been, and sensed it was better not to talk about it. Instead he repeated his question.

'They wouldn't,' said Charity. 'They'll wait for the gang to move on.'

'Tell me about your religion,' asked Jubal. 'I need to understand your people if I'm going to help them.'

Charity began to speak.

Hope had been founded in the latter half of the 1800s by an off-shoot band of the Quaker faith. Sickened by the violence of what was then the Frontier, Jonathan Hardy had gathered a bunch of like-minded folk around him and headed west to the unspoiled country. The original aim had been to reach Oregon and set up a community there, but the wagon train had strayed off course into Montana. The pioneers got as far as the valley before Winter shut them in. Unable to move on until the snows melted, they had fended as best they could; and found the valley hospitable. When the Spring thaw came, they voted to stay and build their settlement in the high mountains. They were far enough away from any other towns to live their lives the way they wanted. The Nez Perce were friendly and the land was good. There was game in the hills, beaver and otter and fish in the rivers; timber along the hills; grass on the meadows. They built Hope and stayed there. Their credo was peace. At any cost. Twice, wandering parties of Sioux had chanced on the settlement and taken what they wanted. After that, the Indians stopped raiding, bored by the lack of resistance. Now they traded peaceably with the Hopers, and mostly left them alone. They had been alone until Jacob ten Eyck rode in.

The brief history gave Jubal a vague idea. Charity's scratching gave him another.

'Let me see your hand,' he said.

'Why?'

'You've been scratching your wrists. Maybe I can do something for them.'

She looked at him, warily: 'I don't like to be touched.'

'I'm a doctor.' He lifted the medical bag on to the bed to emphasize his words. 'I want to help you.'

Nervously, she extended her arm. Jubal pushed the sleeve of her dress back and stared at the underside of her wrist. There was a ring of small red spots.

He took her left hand: the same ring showed.

When he looked at her face he saw a faint tracery of redness along the hair line.

Despite the warmth of the cabin Jubal felt a sudden chill.

'I'll look at Pieter now,' he said.

'Have I got it?' Charity's voice was both frightened and exultant. 'Will the others have it?'

'I don't know yet.' Jubal's voice was quiet and very careful. 'Let's take a look at Pieter, then I'll tell you.'

They went into the other bedroom.

The air was hot and sickly with the odour of sweat and fever. The man on the big double bed was wrapped up inside the sheets like a restless corpse wound round with stained winding cloths. He couldn't have been much more than twenty years old, but his face was hollowed out, the eyes rimmed with black and sunken inside his face. He muttered in his sleep.

Jubal hauled the blankets back and tugged the sweat-sodden nightshirt away from the body.

Jubal stared at the young outlaw, then bent over the bed. Pieter ten Eyck was covered with ugly red blotches. Around his groin and lower stomach they were merely dark eruptions on the pale flesh. Around his wrists, where he had scratched, they were raw and suppurating. Over his face and neck, extending down to his shoulders, the red marks were thick, pustulous swellings. They broke up the skin and oozed a yellowish liquid from the crusted sores.

Jubal stepped back and asked for hot water.

'Why?' asked Charity.

'He's got smallpox,' said Jubal. 'So have you.'

CHAPTER SEVEN

Smallpox has an incubation period of twelve days. In most cases it kills. The disease is unlike most other killers, in that it tends to strike during the Winter and is horribly contagious. Some people are naturally resistant, but most cases suffering the sickness require strict quarantine for at least sixteen days. Isolation of the victim is vital. So is the burning of all his clothing, bedding, anything with which he has had contact.

After all that, he may live. Probably scarred.

When Jubal looked at Pieter ten Eyck he saw a man in the last throes of the disease. The scabs were joining together over the outlaw's face and his fever was too high for hope to take much place in the diagnosis.

Pieter ten Eyck was dying.

So, most probably, was anyone he had come in contact with since the illness developed.

Jubal washed his hands and face, then asked Charity where she got her water from.

It came out of a well at the rear of the cabin. Jubal set the girl to finding every bucket she could and when they were assembled he told her to bank up the fires in the stove and the hearth and get the water boiling.

Charity was confused. The idea of catching smallpox frightened her, but the idea of transferring the disease to the ten Eyck gang appealed to her. Jubal stared at her, doing his best to batter down the barricades of vengeful madness that coloured her thinking.

'Listen,' he said slowly. 'If you get it like that man in there, you'll most likely die. If you live, you'll be walking around with scars on your face for the rest of your life. You're young. You can probably live it out, but there won't be anyone wants to look at you because you'll be too ugly. You want that?'

Charity shook her head. Then she smiled.

'I could kill them that way, couldn't I?'

Jubal shrugged. 'Sure. You could kill them that way. But why? Let me kill them. You live. That's better, isn't it? Anyway, they're probably dying right now. Most likely, they all caught it from Pieter.'

Charity laughed. 'That would be just, like the Bible says. They'll be struck down by their own sins.'

'Yeah,' said Jubal, 'and Hope with them. You want to see your neighbours dying? You willing to kill them to get ten Eyck's gang?'

The argument broke through the shroud of hate clouding Charity's mind. She got the fires banked up while Jubal fetched water.

He was carrying the final bucket into the cabin when someone pounded on the door.

Charity slid the catch loose and the door sprang open. Snow blew in around a tall man dressed in a heavy cloth coat. He wore a wide-brimmed black stetson and a thick beard. He carried a Winchester in his hands.

Jubal set the bucket down and stared at the man. He was around six feet tall and built out to match his height. His cold grey eyes scanned the room and settled on Jubal along with the muzzle of the Winchester.

'What in the goddam hell's goin' on?' he asked. 'Who's this?'

'Cade,' said Jubal. 'Doctor Jubal Cade. You got a smallpox epidemic on your hands.'

Jacob ten Eyck looked suspicious, then doubtful. Then the words sank in and he looked scared.

'Smallpox? Who's got it?'

'Your brother,' grunted Jubal. 'He's dying of it.'

'Oh Christ!' Ten Eyck took a step back before he remembered he didn't know Jubal. 'Pieter?'

Jubal nodded. 'Yeah. Pieter.'

Jacob stayed in the doorway. 'Where'd you come from?'

Jubal played a long gamble. There was no reason for him to be in Hope; except to find the gang. But smallpox was a frightening word, and he could prove his credentials as a doctor if he needed to. He decided to play on natural fear and the reliance of most people on a medical man.

'I'm a doctor,' he said. 'I came in over the mountain after I heard about Kempton.'

Ten Eyck's carbine lifted to front Jubal's chest. 'What the hell you mean?'

'Smallpox,' Jubal repeated. 'Most of Kempton's got it. The town's in quarantine. Got a whole regiment of cavalry round it so no one'll get out. They got thirty dead already. They were burning the bodies when I left.'

'Oh, Jesus Christ!' snarled ten Eyck. 'Fuckin' smallpox.'

Jubal held up his bag. 'I was riding through when the Army told me,' he lied, 'I reckoned you'd need a doctor up here.'

Jacob thought about it for a moment, then: 'How'd you know we'd be here?'

The Winchester levelled up again as doubt entered the outlaw's mind. Jubal thought fast and compounded his lie, building on the original fabric.

'I didn't. I just heard you was headed north, so I rode the same way. Fact is, I was planning to make a practice in Kempton, but they wouldn't let me in. The Army, that was. So I thought I might find work up here. I guess I have.'

Jacob was too worried to concern himself overmuch with the niceties of Jubal's explanation. 'An' we got it?' he asked.

Jubal nodded. 'If that's your brother back there, then sure you got it.'

'Oh, sweet Jesus Christ!' moaned ten Eyck. 'Smallpox!'

Raw fear showed in his eyes and the carbine drooped down and away from Jubal's chest. When next he spoke, his voice was softer, worried.

'How long before I know fer sure?'

Jubal shrugged. 'Depends when Pieter caught it. Maybe a fortnight, maybe longer. I'd need to examine you all to be sure.'

'An' Pieter,' moaned the outlaw, 'he's gonna die?'

'Looks that way,' said Jubal. Bluntly. 'He's all covered with sores like he's got it real bad. The next day or so should tell. He'll live or die. Meanwhile, I'd best stay with him.'

'Yeah,' said ten Eyck. 'You do that. Do the best you can, doc. I'll see you get paid if he lives.'

'Thanks,' said Jubal, 'but that doesn't matter. Like I said I'm a doctor. I took an oath to save life. I'll save his if I can.'

He stepped up to the door and swung it partway shut. 'Keep away. Tell everyone else to do the same. The only way I can hold it in check is if everyone stays isolated.'

He swung the door all the way closed and dropped the latch over. From outside there came the sound of a low moan, then steps receding away from the cabin. After that, just the wind and the soft sound of falling snow.

He had lied only in part. Smallpox was a terrifying disease that could wipe out a community and spread to others with travellers or food or even simple blankets, trade stuff like that. It had been fairly common in England when he was studying medicine there and special hospitals were set up to keep the victims in isolation. At least Hope was apart from any other settlements, so the contagion was unlikely to spread. Provided no one tried to escape. And provided he could hold the cases down while he tended them.

It was a curious situation. He had come to Hope with the clear intention of destroying the ten Eyck gang. Of killing them if he had to for the sake of Hodge's reward and the chance of finding Kincaid. Now he was determined to nurse them through and worry about the reward after. It was instinctive and inevitable; a natural part of his being, assumed when he took the Hippocratic Oath that demanded he save life when and where he could. Even if he snuffed it out later.

He turned back to the fire, where Charity waited with wide eyes and a trembling, frightened mouth.

'You got a wash-tub?' he asked.

'There's a bath-house behind the cabin.'

'Fill it up with hot water,' he said. 'Strip off and leave your clothes outside. Can you get more?' She nodded. 'Good. Burn everything you got. Burn what you're wearing and everything else you've touched since Pieter came here. Take your bedding and burn that, too. Everything.'

The girl nodded, her hatred of the gang suddenly overcome by the greater fear. 'What about Pieter's stuff?'

'I'll handle that,' said Jubal. 'You just go do what I told you.'

She scurried out with a bucket of boiling water. Jubal yawned and glanced at the half-hunter. It was three in the morning.

He took off his jacket and his vest, rolled up his sleeves and let out a long, slow sigh. There wasn't an awful lot he could do, except try to keep the contagion inside reasonable bounds.

And hope he didn't catch it.

He went back to Pieter's room and gathered up the outlaw's clothes. Bundling them together, he carried them outside and tossed them on to the piling snow. He took the guns and the saddlebags, then stripped the bed and added all of that to the pile. There was kerosene inside the cupboard in the cabin's main room. It burned even with the wind blowing snow over the flames. Then he dressed the bed again and examined his patient.

Pieter ten Eyck's pulse was weak, fluttering in rapid beats and overlong stops. Jubal washed him down and cleaned the sores as best he could. He stayed with the boy until dawn broke and Jacob came back, knocking on the door like a nervous visitor. By then Charity was bathed and back in bed under fresh linen, sound asleep.

Jubal opened the door and stared out through red-rimmed eyes.

'How is he?' asked Jacob. 'He gonna live?'

Jubal shook his head. 'I don't think so. I've done everything I can, but he was a long way gone before I saw him.'

Jacob's eyes flashed and his hand went down to the Colt on his hip. He opened his mouth to speak, but Jubal got in first.

'You'd best get rid of your stuff, too. Anyone who's come close to him might carry the germs. That's sure death and the only way to lose it is to burn it up.'

It was near enough to the truth to be convincing, and it scared the hell out of Jacob. By the time the rest of Hope woke up there were fires burning all over the settlement.

The outlaw gang shed all of their gear on a big bonfire in the centre of the street. The clothing worn by the women they had taken was added to the blaze, as was the bedding. Jacob agreed to bathe in the river so long as one man stood guard. Jubal examined them in turn. It was the first time he had seen the whole gang up close and he made the most of the opportunity.

Jeb Greenhaugh was a tall, rangy man, his receding hair compensated by a tangling growth that fell down over his shoulders. He was skinny, with nervous blue eyes that darted round as he moved, and long fingers that twitched as though anxious to reach a gun.

Jimmy Schwatz was short and blond. His face was sallow, with a narrow jaw and a sharp nose that gave him a ferrety look. He wore a beard the same colour as his stringy hair, and he laughed a lot. Too much.

Ten Eyck was dark as his brother was fair, a big, muscular man with scars across his back and the kind of eyes that chill people with their cold stare.

When they were done with the bathing Jubal had them send their women into the water. Then the rest of the Hopers. There were only twenty people left, nine of them men between the ages of sixteen and forty, the rest female.

There was an argument about the women showing their bodies that Jubal overcame with threats about the danger of the disease and cajoling of the outlaws. The result was that ten Eyck and the others got dressed and stood with their backs to the river as Jubal watched the ladies go in.

There were eleven women counting five little girls of no more than nine or ten.

When they were all bathed and dressed in fresh clothes Jubal checked the bonfires. The snow had stopped falling and a thick pall of smoke hung over Hope. The wind shifted it about when it got higher than the low roofs of the cabins and blew it away to the west where it broke up and scattered across the faces of the hills.

Jubal checked them one by one.

He had never experienced a smallpox case before, and his knowledge was based on theoretical study in England. Ten Eyck and Schwatz showed signs of the disease, and two women complained of aching backs and running noses. Jubal suggested that they keep away from the others, backing his argument against Jacob's disagreement with the threat of counter-infection. The result was that the Hopers were herded into their church with bedding and food, guarded by two of the outlaws.

Schwatz and Greenhaugh took the first turn. Ten Eyck went back with Jubal to check his brother.

Pieter was worse. And so was Charity. The rash was spreading over her face, the blotches getting larger and more violent. She complained of aches and swollen glands, and her face was covered with a fine sheening of perspiration despite the cold.

Jacob ten Eyck looked at her and turned to Jubal.

'You reckon she's got it?' he asked. 'She caught the pox off'n Pieter?'

Jubal shoved the girl inside the cabin and turned back to the big outlaw.

'She has to have it,' said Jubal. 'She's been in contact with him since you got here. If she doesn't die from it, she'll have carried it around. That's why I wanted everyone to get cleaned up.'

'I figgered that,' grunted ten Eyck. 'Pieter an' her, they must be the ones could spread it.'

Jubal nodded, wondering what the outlaw was getting at.

'I was in Deadwood once,' said Jacob. 'They had it there. Killed off most of the kids.'

'It usually does,' said Jubal. 'It's mostly kids get it. Under the age of ten. If they live, they're usually immune.'

'What's that mean?' said ten Eyck. 'Immune?'

'Means they don't catch it again,' answered Jubal. 'The germ gets killed off and the body knows how to handle it again.'

Jacob nodded and stared away at the mountains.

After a bit he turned back to Jubal and said: 'So if I caught it in Deadwood an' I lived it through, I'd be all right now?'

Jubal nodded.

'We was all there,' grunted Jacob. 'Me an' Pieter. Jeb an' Jimmy. Hiram, too, only he's dead, I guess. Back in Kempton.'

'Pieter could be the carrier,' said Jubal. 'It happens that way sometimes. A man can get the disease and live through it, but it stays with him. He passes it on without getting sick himself. He gives it to other people and rides clear. Then it can hit him.'

'An' you reckon it was that way with Pieter?' asked Jacob. 'He's been sick all along without me knowin' it?'

Jubal shrugged. 'Could be. I don't have the equipment to find out. You'd need a proper hospital for that.'

'But you reckon only me an' Jimmy got it now?' said ten Eyck.

'Yeah,' said Jubal. 'You've got the signs, so does Schwatz. The next few days will tell if you're immune, or not.'

'But Pieter could be the one brought it on?' Jacob repeated. 'An' that girl has it bad on account o' bein' in there with him all this time.'

'She's got it,' said Jubal patiently, 'but she could live through it. It needs time to find out.'

'I don't like waitin' on a thing like that,' grunted Jacob. 'Not even fer my brother.'

'There's not much else you can do,' said Jubal. 'He'll live or die, like Charity.'

'But if he lives,' Jacob struggled to make the point, 'he could still carry it with him?'

Jubal nodded again. 'Sure. Anytime.'

'Shit!' snarled Jacob. 'That goddamn little bastard. Jesus Christ! He mighta killed me!'

He reached inside his coat and hauled out a Colt's Frontier model. 'Charity!' he shouted. 'Get on out here, girl. Right now!'

'What you doing?' said Jubal. 'Leave her be.'

'Close yore goddam mouth, doc,' snarled ten Eyck. 'You said the best way to stop it was to kill it off at the source.'

Understanding dawned on Jubal and he powered forwards at the bigger man. Ten Eyck swung the Colt up and across, smashing the barrel hard against the side of Jubal's head. The smaller man groaned and fell away. Jacob kicked him in the belly, then swung the Colt down in a vicious arc that slammed Jubal's face into the snow.

Charity Lambert appeared at the door.

Jacob ten Eyck shot her dead centre of her stomach. The bullet went in through the covering of cloth and skin and muscle. It tore through her belly and came out behind, doubling her over and pitching her back inside the cabin. Charity slumped over the planks with blood spilling from her mouth and midriff. She tried to speak, but only blood came out, thick and warm over her lips. Jacob stepped up on to the porch and fired again. The second shot drilled a third eye between the staring, pain-filled, orbs. Charity's head slammed against the bare planks, spilling blood and bone and brains in a sticky pool.

Jacob ten Eyck stepped over the body and kicked the door of his brother's room open.

Pieter was huddled inside a cocoon of blankets. He was shaking and sweating, and his face was ugly with weeping sores.

Jacob stared at him for a moment, then thumbed the hammer of the Colt and levelled the gun on Pieter's face.

Pieter sat up. Sweat ran down his cheeks and his eyes were drawn back inside black, blank holes of red raw flesh.

'Jacob?' he mumbled. 'That you, Jacob?'

'Yeah,' grunted ten Eyck. 'It's me. Yore big brother.'

'Give me a drink,' moaned Pieter. 'I got a thirst on me. I need a drink.'

'You drink all you want,' rasped Jacob. 'If you can find it where you're goin'.'

'What you mean, Jacob?' Pieter stared at the doorway. He blinked a few times, and wiped a hand over his face. The hand was marked with sores. 'I don't understand.'

'You got the pox,' grunted Jacob. 'You been carryin' it with you. I can't afford that, boy. Not even fer you.'

Pieter got his eyes focussed and saw the gun in his brother's hand.

'Why you pointin' that my way?' he asked. 'What for?'

'Gonna kill you, boy,' said Jacob. 'It's the only way.'

Pieter opened his mouth to scream, but Jacob's bullet shut off the sound. It went through Pieter's teeth and snapped his neck. His head thudded back against the wood of the wall. Blood spilled over his chin and two thick streams gouted from his nostrils.

Jacob fired again.

His brother was staring at him out of wide, empty eyes.

The second bullet hit Pieter in the chest and hurled him back, then forwards. The third shattered his descending skull, smashing the top of the cranium and emerging from between his shoulders.

Jacob groaned and emptied the gun into the corpse.

Then he stumbled out of the cabin, shaking his head.

He looked down at Jubal, who was lifting up from the snow, rubbing at the bruise along his cheek and the swelling lump on the back of his head.

'I guess I contained it,' muttered Jacob. 'Leastways, I done the best I could think of.'

Jubal shook his head and got his hands under his chest. Slowly, he eased upwards. He was tired and hurting and the pain of the blows did nothing to help his attention or his weariness.

'What the hell d'you mean?' he mumbled. 'What did you do?'

'Shot them,' said ten Eyck. 'Pieter an' the girl. I figgered we'd cut the pox off at the source.'

Jubal got up on his knees and let his head droop. The snow was cold and clean and white. A whole lot cleaner than people.

'You killed them?' he groaned. 'You mean you shot the girl and your own brother?'

'Sure,' said Jacob. 'I didn't have much choice.'

Jubal rubbed snow over his face and tried to ignore the pain in his skull. 'You didn't have to kill them,' he groaned.

'It was on yore word,' said ten Eyck. 'Doctor's orders.'

CHAPTER EIGHT

It was a miserable Christmas for the citizens of Hope.

The ten Eyck gang held them inside the church, grudgingly allowing Jubal to check them over twice a day, and giving them food only when Jubal argued.

Jubal himself had forgotten that it was the season of good-will, and found it difficult to muster any more feeling than a weary determination to do what he could on behalf of the citizens. That wasn't very much. His medical supplies were tailored more to the exigencies of gunshot wounds or broken limbs than to tending smallpox victims. And the victims began to show.

It was Christmas Eve when the first child went down with the sickness. She was a little girl of nine years, fair-haired and frightened of the rash that appeared on her face and hands. Jubal found her in the morning, feverish and complaining of an aching back. He asked Jacob to let him isolate the child and her parents in their cabin, but the outlaw refused.

'You said to contain it, doc,' he grunted, 'an' that's what I'm doin'. I'm gonna contain it in that goddam church until I know we're safe.'

Jubal tried to persuade the Dutchman, but ten Eyck stayed obstinate.

'Lissen, doc,' he said. 'You told me the only way to be sure o' not spreadin' it was to keep a tight lid on the damn' thing. That's what I'm doin', whether you like it or not.'

Jubal gave up. Ten Eyck had taken his weapons and threatened to burn the church if Jubal tried to escape: all he could do was try to keep the fever down and hope the girl lived through it.

That night he was stretched out on the sofa in the Lambert cabin, sipping coffee and worrying, when he heard the sound of voices. He stood up and opened the door. The night was still and clear, empty of snow and a little warmer than the last few

67

days. The sky was clear and velvet blue, pricked out with tiny points of light. Jeb Greenhaugh was standing outside the church, cradling a rifle in his arms and blowing streamers of condensation from his muffler-wrapped lips. Up the street, Jacob ten Eyck and Jimmy Schwatz were drinking apple brandy and eating roasted pork from the cabin's supplies. A faint glow showed through the boarded-up windows of the church. It was accompanied by the sound of voices.

Jubal stood listening, trying to make out the words.

Silent night, holy night,
All is calm, all is bright . . .

Greenhaugh turned away from the door. He had his rifle up ready to pound the butt against the wood. Jubal watched him lower the gun and step down off the porch. Slowly, dragging his feet, the outlaw walked away from the church.

The tune changed.

Once in royal David's city,
In a lowly cattle shed . . .

Greenhaugh saw Jubal watching and changed direction. He came over to the cabin and paused. Jubal saw that his eyes were moist. Greenhaugh shrugged, dragging a gloved hand over his face.

'Been a long time since I heard anything like that, doc,' he muttered. 'It kinda does things to a feller's gut. I remember my maw used to sing that one.'

The carol changed again.

O, little town of Bethlehem,
How still we see thee lie . . .

'Jesus!' said Greenhaugh. 'I wish we never come here. I wish we'd stayed south.'

'It's not too late to leave,' Jubal said. 'You don't have the pox. You could go now.'

Greenhaugh shook his head. 'No I couldn't. Jacob'd never allow it. He'd come after me, an' I ain't willin' to chance that. He's a mean man, doc. You remember that.'

'I know,' said Jubal. 'It takes a mean man to shoot his own brother.'

Greenhaugh shrugged. 'Yeah. I didn't like that myself. But I ain't ready to argue with Jacob. I ain't ready to lissen to them carols, neither. I'm gonna go get me a drink. Don't try anythin', will you? I'd hate to shoot you.'

Jubal shook his head and watched the outlaw pace down the snow-packed street. The door of ten Eyck's cabin opened and Greenhaugh stepped inside. The night was still calm and clear and clean.

Away in a manger,
A crib for his bed ...

The words suddenly faded away, replaced by a scream. Jubal grabbed his valise and ran towards the outlaws' cabin. Ten Eyck gave him the key to the church and sent Greenhaugh back with him. They opened the door and went inside.

The little girl with the fair hair was dead. The scream belonged to her mother.

The woman was kneeling in the centre of the aisle, facing the altar with her daughter's body cradled in her arms. She was rocking backwards and forwards, spilling tears over the empty eyes of her child. A dark-haired man knelt beside her, weeping as he touched the hair of his wife and the face of his daughter. The others stood in a nervous semicircle, unsure of going forwards to comfort the grieving parents or stay clear of the infection.

Jubal checked the child's pulse: it was still. He looked at her face and then felt her stomach. She was into the early stages of the disease, but her death was caused as much by malnutrition as by the smallpox.

'I'm sorry, ma'am,' he said wearily, 'but I have to take her away. I have to bury her.'

Greenhaugh shoved his rifle up against the woman's face as she tried to hold her child back. Then clubbed the man as he sprang up fighting.

Jubal took the small body and carried it out of the church.

'I want my baby back!' screamed the mother.

'She's dead, ma'am,' Jubal said from the doorway. 'I'm sorry, but you can't look back.'

He carried the tiny corpse out into the street and set it on the still-burning fire. Ten Eyck and Schwatz came out from their cabin and watched as Greenhaugh slopped kerosene over the smouldering wood. Flames leaped up into the night. The church went quiet. The street filled up with the stink of burning cloth, then the sickly odour of roasting flesh.

'Oh, Jesus,' said Greenhaugh, 'I never thought it'd be like this.'

'Come an' get a drink, Jeb,' ten Eyck shouted. 'You look like you need it. You, too, doc.'

Jubal shook his head. The cabin door closed, leaving the street empty, save for the fire and the solitary figure watching the blaze.

The flames lit up the frontages of the empty cabins. Sparks flew high in the still air, crackling as they hit the colder level above the roof. Atop the bonfire, Jubal could see the outline of a small body. And almost taste the sticky sweetness of the smell.

He waited until the corpse was totally consumed by the flames, then walked slowly back to the Lambert cabin. He got back inside and glanced at his watch. The gold half-hunter glistened in the light of the kerosene lanterns. It was nine minutes after midnight.

On Christmas day.

In the morning two more people died.

One was a sixteen-year-old boy, the other a sixty-year-old grandfather.

Three women followed them the next day.

Between that time and the New Year, four more of the children died, and two more men.

There was nothing Jubal could do except ease the sick as best he could and make sure the bodies were burned. Ten Eyck left him to handle it with Greenhaugh's assistance. The balding outlaw, like Jubal himself, seemed immune to the disease. He even seemed stirred by some last vestiges of conscience as he hefted the corpses from the church and slung them on the fire that was now a permanent feature of Hope's street.

Ten Eyck and Jimmy Schwatz developed nothing more than bad fevers that they fought with liquor and better food than the owners of it got. After three weeks, Jubal was as confident as he could be that the epidemic was controlled.

The population of Hope was reduced to eight people. There were five men left, and three women. All of the children were dead, and the eight survivors were gaunt with hunger and near mad with fear.

When Jacob was sure there would be no more outbreaks, he let the people free of the church and gathered them in the street.

'Lissen!' he hollered. 'I know you folks want to see us gone, so I'm givin' you the chance. I ain't overly keen to stay round this place, but I ain't got no way to move out. Leastways, not across the mountains. Way I figger it is that you can build us a raft an' we'll go down the river. Anyone know where it heads to?'

An old man Jubal had come to know stepped forwards. His name was William Tenneker and he had been a trapper before joining the community of Hope.

'Foller the stream down,' he said in a wheezy voice, 'an' you'll reach the Clearwater. That'll take you into the Snake River. After that you can fork off to Oregon or Idaho, whichever you fancy.'

'Draw us a map,' said ten Eyck. 'An' make sure you do it good.'

The map was produced that evening. Ten Eyck called Jubal in to study it.

'Why?' Jubal asked. 'I don't know this country, and you'll not be taking me with you.'

Ten Eyck chuckled, 'Think agin, doc. Way I see it is that those bastards'd foul up any raft they built fer me. If they know you're comin' along with us, an' they know you'll get yore feet wet if it fouls up, they'll build it right. They feel kinda indebted to you, so they'll take extra care.'

'You're crazy,' said Jubal. 'The river's bad enough now. Adding more weight is just chancing a spill.'

'You better hope not,' grinned ten Eyck, 'because you're comin' with us, like it or not.'

71

The next day they began to build the raft.

The river was around fifteen feet wide where it passed by Hope, and some seven to ten feet deep. The raft was built of timbers salvaged from the cabins and tin drums emptied of oil or kerosene or whatever had been inside. It took shape slowly, put together by the unwilling citizens under the watchful gaze of the outlaws.

It was comprised of flat timbers, cross-strutted with planks that were nailed down on to the base and then roped on for extra protection. Drums were sealed up with pitch and lashed at the corners, two more along each side. A kind of bulwark was nailed on at the front and a skeleton of poles built up at the rear and covered with a canvas awning. There was a big steering paddle mounted between two uprights at the tail and poles and oars stowed along the sides. Each flank of the raft was raised a foot or more above the waterline, and the whole thing was caulked with pitch above and below.

It took a week to build and when it was finished ten Eyck called the Hopers together in the street.

'You folks done us real proud,' he sneered, 'an' we enjoyed yore hospitality this Christmas. We'll be leavin' you soon, so I wanted to say thanks. After we're gone, you just remember that we'll have the doc with us. Anythin' that happens to us is gonna happen to him, too. If the raft spills, he's gonna drown like the rest o' us. If there's anyone comes chasin', he'll be in the firin' line. You remember that. The best thing you can do is keep silent an' watch us go. Now get the fuckin' thing in the water.'

There was food stowed under the canvas and a supply of weapons and cartridges. Jubal's Spencer was in amongst the baggage, though ten Eyck let him keep his handgun. Unloaded. The horses were left behind and the last items the gang loaded on board were the sacks of money taken from the Kempton bank.

Jubal went on board under the wary eyes of ten Eyck and Schwatz, the worried gaze of Greenhaugh.

'You're crazy,' he said as they pushed off. 'You'll never make it.'

'Shut up,' snarled Jacob ten Eyck. 'You don't have no choice. You just got sold down the river.'

CHAPTER NINE

Ten Eyck manned the steering oar while Greenhaugh poled them off from the bank and Schwatz called directions from the prow.

The raft eased out into the current and began to drift westwards. The bulk of the platform was sufficient to maintain a reasonable degree of stability, and the sealed drums and caulked timbers kept the main part of it clear of the water and dry. The river was running too fast to allow any real concentrations of ice to build up, though floating chunks drifted past, knocking against the raft as they swirled by. To either side, the river's banks were heavy with snow. Curling lips of ice hung over the water, extending beyond the edges of the dark earth like frozen waves. Beneath the glistening rims the soil was eroded away by the flow of the water, held firm under the snow's weight by the solidifying process of winter. It was too cold for the snow to have added any appreciable increase to the river's volume and while it ran fast, it was still navigable.

Hope faded away behind them as they entered the canyon Jubal had seen when first he rode in. The rock walls lifted up sheer on either side, hung with icicles and bare-limbed bushes.

The stone was mostly bare, reaching down like a grey curtain that got black and slick where it met the river. The effect was that of a funnel, channelling the water into a tighter area so that it ran faster, becoming turbulent where rocks thrust up from the bed. Jimmy Schwatz's shouting became more urgent as he called warnings of the obstacles, and Jubal took the second paddle, ready to add his weight should a crash threaten.

Twice they scraped past boulders that might have ripped their vessel apart. Then the canyon straightened out and they picked up speed, heading straight-on for a seemingly blank wall of rock.

At the last moment, when it seemed impossible they could do anything other than ram headlong into the stone, the river bent northwards. It funnelled out through an overhung gorge where the rock came down and brushed the sides of the raft. Jubal crouched down, holding the paddle like a lance that he stabbed at the unyielding stone when it looked like smashing them into flinders. It was hard, muscle-aching work, and the vista of rock became blurred by their speed. Details got hidden behind a foaming spill of white water and slurred, shining stone. The air filled up with the roaring of the river and the shouts of ten Eyck.

Then the gorge opened up and the river got wider. The naked rock gave way to snow-fields dotted with trees and the banks became flat again, stretching away on both sides across empty spaces of blinding brilliance. Floes of four and five feet drifted lazily across their path, slowing their progress so that Jubal and Greenhaugh were forced to join Schwatz at the head of the raft and pole a path clear.

By nightfall they were, Jubal estimated, some thirty or forty miles downstream.

Ahead, the river opened up and tiny coves showed along the banks. Ten Eyck steered them in to the south side as twilight came down. There was a section of the bank cut through by some earlier flood, leaving an oxbow loop of calmer water surrounding a tiny island. The deep edges of the spill were close enough to touch as they steered in, and the island hung pines over the off-shoot like a canopy. Around the curve was a natural wharf where the banks on both sides had got eroded away and tumbled down into the water. The channel narrowed out and got shallow enough that they could step off the raft on to dry land. Muddy, and cold, but welcoming in comparison with the main branch.

Ten Eyck let the raft drift in and ground on the overspill, then shouted for Greenhaugh and Schwatz to plant mooring lines.

Jubal followed the big outlaw up on to the island and watched as the other men hammered pegs into the soil and looped ropes from the raft to the halters.

Ten Eyck was grinning.

'I ain't steered a boat since I left Missouri,' he said. 'It's a good feelin'. Let's a man know he's doin' somethin'.'

'You did plenty in Hope,' Jubal grunted. 'Kempton, too.'

Ten Eyck looked at him and chuckled. 'Killin', you mean? Lissen, doc,' he stared at the halter-lines, then: 'I got raised in a Dutch community. My paw and my maw were immigrants. Flemish Dutch. Walloons. They scraped their savin's together to buy passage over here an' when they reached the Liberty Land all they got was trod on. They spent ten years an' all their money settin' up a store. Paw signed some mortgage paper to buy it. He couldn't meet a couple o' the payments so the bank foreclosed on him. He sold his gear an' bought hisself passage on a train headin' west. My maw got killed by the Sioux an' my paw died of the fever exactly nine miles west o' the Missouri River. I was just thirteen years old.' He chuckled. 'Hell! I didn't figger to carve no home outta the goddam wilderness an' I didn't take to bein' fostered out, so I quit the train. Got me a job on a river barge. Was a good time, that. We worked the Missouri from Bismarck to Kansas City. That's how I know about handlin' river craft.'

Jubal shivered in the cold air. There was nothing unusual in ten Eyck's story, nothing so far that might not apply to hundreds of decent citizens. But it was the first time the big outlaw had talked at any length, and somewhere along the line he might just mention something Jubal could use against him.

'So how'd you get on the wrong side of the law?' he asked.

Ten Eyck grinned. 'I allus did have a temper. Pieter was with me, seein' as how I was all he had by way of family. He grew up on the river. Then some ole biddy in St Joseph said he should go into an orphanage. Tried to split us up. We was all set to run away when they sent a deputy to fetch us in. I put a blade in his gut an' we cut out fer New Orleans. Was some trouble there with a feller thought the ace came off the bottom o' the deck. I shot him, so we was runnin' again. We headed fer Texas an' worked a ranch a spell. The foreman never did take to me, an' one time he picked a fight. I killed him. Bastard rancher said he was gonna turn me in, so I shot him, too.

'Since then we been runnin' more or less permanent. Wasn't no one ever did us any favours, so we figgered not to do them any. Hittin' the odd stage looked to be the easiest way to make a livin', so we took a few. Met Jimmy an' Hiram that way.

Hiram's dead now, o' course. Back in Kempton. Then Jeb kinda teamed up with us an' we ran pretty wild.'

He broke off, staring at the river. They had been walking while Jacob spoke, and now were on the far side of the island, out of earshot of the others.

'Guess you think I was pretty mean back there, shootin' Pieter an' all.'

Jubal nodded. 'It didn't look exactly like brotherly love.'

'Mebbe not,' grunted ten Eyck. 'I guess I did go kinda crazy fer a spell, but when I saw his face an' I knew he was dyin' I figgered it'd be best if he went quick.'

'Like shooting a sick dog,' murmured Jubal bitterly.

'Yeah, that's it.' Ten Eyck sounded almost enthusiastic. 'I'm glad you understand, doc.'

Jubal glanced at him. Opened his mouth to argue, but then thought better of it. If the outlaw believed he understood — maybe even approved — then perhaps his guard would drop some. Perhaps this curious granting of confidence might allow Jubal a chance to escape.

'Don't go tellin' the others any o' that.' The outlaw's voice got cold again. 'That stuff's all private. Don't rightly understand why I told you, except you bein' a doctor makes it kinda different.'

No, Jubal thought, *it doesn't make it different at all. It still makes you a killer. It doesn't change anything.*

Ten Eyck interrupted the thought. 'Let's get back. We'd best get a fire goin' while we still got some light.'

They built a fire and settled down to eat. Then they set their bedrolls out and Schwatz tied Jubal's wrists and ankles together. It was a cold, uncomfortable night.

The next few days carried them steadily westwards and south through stretches of river alternately creamed white with tumbling foam or thick with piled-up ice. Twice they grounded on rocks and came close to wrecking the raft on the jagged boulders sticking up like teeth from the white-water rapids. Three times Jubal and Schwatz and Greenhaugh were forced to struggle on to the banks and haul the raft by means of drag lines over barriers of floating ice. It was back-breaking work that left them all bone-weary at the end of the day, too exhausted to do anything other than cook some food and collapse into their blankets.

By now they were well into the upper curve of the Clearwater, drifting down the centre of the Columbia Plateau. Ahead lay Lewiston, on the border of Montana and Washington. There the Clearwater fed into the Snake and, according to Tenneker's description, they would have to leave the raft. The headwaters of the Salmon River converged on the Snake just west of Lewiston, then swelled as it ran westwards into the great Columbia, gathering speed and force on its headlong rush to the Pacific coast.

Jubal began to wonder what ten Eyck had planned for him when they hit civilization again.

It seemed unlikely the outlaw would try to keep Jubal under guard in a place the size of Lewiston. It was impossible that he would turn his prisoner free: even though he might not be wanted in the Washington territory, the law might well hold him on Jubal's word. The alternative seemed obvious. If ten Eyck couldn't hold Jubal and couldn't let him go, he would kill him.

The prospect nagged at Jubal's mind as they drew steadily closer to Lewiston. Yet the more he thought about it, the more the problem appeared insoluble. By day he was under the constant gaze of all three killers with nowhere to go except into the river. He doubted he could reach the bank before a bullet or the freezing water claimed his life.

It was Jacob ten Eyck who first brought the whole thing into the open.

They were camped in a stand of pines, the tall trees cutting off the wind as the four men huddled round the fire, drying out their clothing. The river was widened out and relatively calm. According to Tenneker's map they were due to reach Lewiston within the next two days.

Ten Eyck filled his mug with steaming coffee and stared hard in Jubal's direction. His eyes were calculating, studying the smaller man with the cold intensity of a wolf sizing up a wounded elk. Jubal reached forwards to fill his own mug. Jimmy Schwatz was squatting a few feet to his right, Jeb Greenhaugh was seated beside ten Eyck. Jubal decided to hurl

77

the coffee in Jacob's face if it looked like the outlaw was going to draw on him. After that he would try for Schwatz and hope he could get hold of a gun before they shot him.

'There ain't far to go now,' said ten Eyck, 'before we hit town.'

'Thank God,' grunted Greenhaugh. 'I seen enuff river to last me a fair spell.'

'Means we got a problem, though,' murmured the leader. 'What we gonna do with the doc, here?'

Schwatz stroked his scattergun. 'Kill him,' he said. 'What else?'

'No!' Greenhaugh sounded like he meant it. 'He done plenty to help us. Might be, we'd all be dead if it weren't fer him.'

'Kill him,' Schwatz repeated. 'He knows too much. He gets into Lewiston an' opens his mouth, we're all of us dead.'

'That's true,' said ten Eyck thoughtfully. 'But Jeb's got a point.'

'So've I,' rasped Schwatz. 'I wanta stay alive an' free.'

Greenhaugh looked at Jubal. The cold and the rigours of the journey had thinned his face out even more than usual and he was snuffling a cold into his damp beard. He looked worried.

'Christ! Jacob, remember what he done fer Pieter. He tended the boy like a real doc.'

'His duty,' said Schwatz, grinning. 'Ain't that right, doc? You take some kinda oath, don't you? Like a lawman?'

'Hypocritic Oath,' said ten Eyck.

'Hippocratic,' Jubal corrected. 'It says I got a duty to anyone who gets sick.'

'He mighta caught the pox hisself,' ventured Greenhaugh. 'He took that chance.'

'Yeah.' Jacob glanced at Jimmy Schwatz, then back at Jubal. 'I guess he did.'

There was a long silence. Jubal eased sideways, getting his legs under him ready to move. The sound of the hammers on Schwatz's scattergun clicking back was unnaturally loud.

'Put it down, Jimmy,' rasped ten Eyck. 'I want killin' done, I'll let you know.'

'You ain't turnin' him free?' gasped Schwatz. 'You can't.'

But he lowered the hammers.

'I'll do what I want,' said ten Eyck. 'You think otherwise, you stand up an' fight me. Now shut your mouth an' lissen.'

Jubal stayed tense. Jacob stared at him.

'I'm gonna let you go, doc,' he said slowly. 'Not in Lewiston, because we can't take that kinda risk. Way I got things figgered, we should be there by nightfall tomorrow, maybe the next day. Come noonday tomorrow, we'll put you ashore. We'll leave you some gear: yore guns an' yore bag, that kinda stuff. Least enuff to give you a chance. You follow the river down an' you'll reach the town. That's the best I can do on account o' Pieter.'

Schwatz spat into the fire. 'Then what? If he makes it in, he's gonna have a mob o' vigilantes after us.'

Ten Eyck shook his head. 'Time he walks there, we'll be gone. I looked at some maps back in Hope, an' it just happens the Union Pacific's got a line runnin' close to Lewiston. There's a branch line connects the town to the main tracks. The snow's been holdin' off long enuff fer the rails to be open, so we can hop a train an' be long gone afore the doc here walks in.'

'If I can,' rasped Jubal. 'That's a long way on foot.'

Ten Eyck shrugged. 'Best I can do. Beats lettin' Jimmy gun you down, don't it?'

'I'll tell you,' said Jubal. 'The next time I see you.'

Ten Eyck laughed. 'You remember that sayin', doc? About jumpin' outta the fry pan into the fire?'

Jubal nodded, taking the hint.

'Yeah,' he said. Then, too low to be heard: 'But it can't be much worse than stepping out of the river into the snow.'

CHAPTER TEN

They set him down on the north bank the next day. Jacob was true to his word and left the basics of survival piled on the snow. Then they shoved off and disappeared around a curve.

Jubal checked over the gear.

His rifle was there along with a box of cartridges. There was a second box of .45 shells for the Colt. His valise, a canvas groundsheet, and three blankets. Matches. A sack of dried meat, a Bowie knife, a billycan. A bag of coffee and a mug. A length of rope. Greenhaugh had tossed in a set of flannels and two pairs of woollen socks.

Jubal built a fire.

When it was burning nicely, he spread the canvas over the snow and hurried into the longjohns. Then he pulled on one extra set of socks and got dressed again. His torn buffalo coat had been replaced by a heavy loden with a hood that buttoned almost to his eyes. He brewed up some coffee and set a pan of jerky to heating. While it warmed up he cut several lengths of wood from a stand of aspen.

He chose slender branches that he could bend reasonably easily. When he had enough he carried them back to the fire and settled down to curving the springy wood into two wide loops. These he lashed together with sections of the rope so that he ended up with two circles about a foot and a half across. Then he set thinner pieces of the aspen over the circles, making a grid of wood like a clumsy lattice over the main part of the circles.

Next, he used the Bowie knife to cut large pieces from the canvas, of a size to cover the aspen loops above and below. He used the knife to gouge holes through the tough material, and then worked the plaited rope apart so that a section some ten or twelve feet long split up into strands. The rope was of hemp, and each strand was waxed. He used them to tie the cross-struts in place. Then he folded the canvas over both sides of the wood and worked the strands of hemp through the holes to fasten it all in place.

Finally, he cut four holes in a rectangle at the centre of each device and ran more hemp through so that the discs of canvas-covered wood might be fastened to his boots.

It all took the remainder of the day, but when he was finished he had a pair of serviceable snowshoes that would carry him over the soft drifts.

There was barely enough canvas left to form a groundsheet, and that night he shivered inside his blankets while wolves howled too close to the river to let him sleep comfortably.

He stoked up on food before sleeping and again in the morning. The cold woke him before dawn and he ate while the sun came out and set the snow to shining. Then he gathered his supplies together inside one of the blankets and fashioned a rough sack that he hung on his back with the remainder of the rope. He tied the snowshoes to his boots and set off across the white wilderness. His final action before kicking the fire over with snow was to smear charcoal from a burned-down stick over his cheeks and eyelids.

Then he set off.

The river curved between high walls of snow-covered rock, twisting in a serpentine pattern that took long hours of forced travelling out of his journey time. A single hour on the water could carry a raft as much as fifteen or twenty miles. For a man on foot, it was a long, slow trek down the bank, one that might take him a full day to cover the distance a raft got through in a few hours.

It took Jubal three days to reach Lewiston, and when he came in sight of the town he could scarcely see it for the snow dazzle. His face was cracked and raw from the wind and his eyes were squinted up and near-blind from the glare.

Somewhere along the way he killed a rabbit and used its body fats to grease his face. He shot a careless pronghorn, too, which gave him the food he needed and more fat to counter the snow's burning. He used its sinews to reinforce the fastenings of his snowshoes, and the deer's hide to make an extra covering at night.

It was too difficult to carry the meat, so he ate as much as he could and then gathered up the blood-soaked snow and fastened it inside the stomach sac. The snow melted while he stumbled on, but when he got thirsty he sucked on the stinking intestines and drew nourishment from the mixture of blood and water.

He stumbled into Lewiston with a beard frozen hard against his face and frostbite threatening to nip off his feet and fingers and nose.

He was unconscious for two more days.

The first thing he said when he came to was: 'Jacob ten Eyck, where is he?'

The woman tending him shook her head and smiled and pushed him back against the pillows. They were warm and soft, so he went back to sleep, dreaming of white fields where men with pockmarks laughed and shot him down.

The next time he woke he saw that he was inside a room. Covered with fresh white sheets and a layer of blankets that cut off his view of anything bar the window frosted over with ice and the blank expanse of the ceiling.

After that he had a vague memory of someone with gold-rimmed glasses checking over his hands and injecting something into his left arm. Then a dim routine of hot soup and blanket baths delivered by a grey-haired woman with lines on her face and a thin, puckered-in mouth.

One day he felt hands hauling him to a sitting position and opened his eyes on the same face.

The mouth smiled and suddenly looked open and not at all puckered.

'I'm Sarah James,' it said. 'Can you hear me?'

'Yes,' said Jubal. He was surprised at the loudness of his voice; it sounded like a shout. 'Yes, I can.'

'Good. We thought you were dying.'

'No.' He tried to shake his head, but the effort was too much. 'I can't. I have to find them.'

'Eat.' The voice was warm and calm. 'Get some solid food inside you. Then you can talk.'

The food was a stew of beef and beans. He ate it hungrily. Then went back to sleep.

He had no way of knowing when he woke again, except that

82

it must be day because the sun was shining in through the window and there was a bird singing just outside. He sat up and shook his head.

'Take it easy, son,' said a quiet voice from the far end of the bed.

Jubal hiked up on the pillows and saw the gold-rimmed glasses again. They seemed to spring out from under bushy white brows that were the colour of the snow he remembered. Behind the glass two blue eyes twinkled like a Summer sky set between peaks of white brows and moustache.

'I'm Doctor Lewis James,' said the face. 'I reckon you'll be on your feet in a day or so.'

'You found me?' asked Jubal. 'How long ago?'

'No one found you,' said James. 'You walked in. Come straight down mainstreet with snowshoes on your feet. Don't you remember?'

Jubal shook his head. It hurt, so he stopped.

James chuckled. It was a deep, reassuring sound.

'You walked in and went up to the marshal's office. When he asked what you wanted, you told him you were looking for three fellers. Tried to shoot him when he said he couldn't understand you. That was on account of your mouth being pretty well froze up. You couldn't shoot him because you fell down when you took your gloves off. He carried you over to my place and you've been here since then.'

'How long?' Jubal repeated.

'Ten days,' said James calmly. 'It's been seven since the fellers you want quit town.'

'How d'you know?' said Jubal rudely. 'Why didn't anyone stop them?'

'Son,' said James, 'we couldn't help but know you was after them. You hardly spoke of nothing else. You said their names and you told us what they looked like.' His face grimaced as though he tasted something bitter in his mouth. 'You told us what they done, too. We'd have sent word, but all the lines are down. We couldn't stop them because they lit out on the first train south. That was seven days ago, like I said.'

'Where?' Jubal asked.

'South,' said James, 'that's all I know. They could've taken the line off to Portland, or down to the South Pass. It's anyone's guess.'

'No,' said Jubal. 'It's my guess. I have to find them. I made a promise.'

'There's no way you can,' said James. 'They could be any-where.'

'I have to try,' said Jubal. 'I have to do that, at least.'

'Son,' said James, 'you need more time in bed. You're not fit to go chasing outlaws. You're still half-starved, and you come through one of the worst Winters we've seen. Rightly speaking, you should be dead. You need rest and care.'

'When's the next train?' Jubal asked.

James sighed; then 'Tomorrow at noon.'

'You got a railroad map?' said Jubal.

There were three ways Jacob ten Eyck and the others might have gone. Jubal spent half the day studying the maps Lewis James brought him, picking the most likely route. Due west to Portland was one choice; after that, the looping branch of the Northern Pacific that ran up to Seattle before hooking east across the northern tip of Idaho into Montana. After that the railroad became the Great Northern and ran straight across Montana into North Dakota, then on to Minnesota and its cul-mination on the western shore of Lake Superior at Duluth. Alternatively, the rails went south from Portland down the flank of the Cascades, heading for Sacramento and Los Angeles on the Southern Pacific lines. Yet again, ten Eyck might have headed for the country he knew best, taking the southeastern fork that ran parallel to the Snake River north of the Great Salt Lake. That route would hook down through Idaho and Oregon into Wyoming where it linked with the Union Pacific and ran east to Nebraska and the junction of the Missouri at Council Bluffs.

There was no way of knowing which track the gang had taken.

Except, perhaps, that one-sided conversation on the ox-bow.

He thought about it as he stared at the map. Where the Union Pacific cut down the southern edge of Wyoming it met the Kansas Pacific at Cheyenne. From there, it headed straight southwards to Denver before hooking east through Colorado along the line of the Smoky Hill River into Kansas and Missouri.

That was the one name that kept cropping up: Missouri. Jacob ten Eyck had grown up on the river. He had mentioned Kansas City. He had talked about New Orleans and Texas. The only way to get that far south in a hurry was via the railroad. The only way to reach anywhere east of the Great Divide was by taking the rails down into Wyoming. The only place to change routes from there was at Cheyenne.

It was a long chance, but the only one Jubal had.

He climbed out of bed and opened the cupboard built into the wall facing him. His clothes were all there so he climbed into them and went looking for Sarah James.

The doctor's wife was shocked to see him on his feet and got him sat down as fast as she could. On the warm side of her kitchen, with a bowl of stew in front of him.

Jubal thanked her and asked if he couldn't pay for his keep.

She shook her head. 'No. Keeping you alive was reward enough. I had a son might have looked like you if he'd lived. He got killed at Shiloh. No more'n eighteen. He was with the medical corps. Got shot down trying to bring a wounded man in. I guess he took after his daddy.'

Jubal didn't know what to say, so he ate his meal in silence and then went out to his room and got his stuff together.

It was all there. His suit was cleaned and pressed. Someone – Sarah, he thought – had even sponged his grey derby and washed out his shirts. His Colt was oiled and loaded. So was the Spencer. The gunbelt was greased, as was the saddle-holster for the rifle. Even his medical bag was polished. And filled with fresh stock. There were two saddlebags set out on the bed, filled up with clean shirts and fresh underclothing; extra shells and a set of wrapped parcels that held pieces of cake and sweet biscuits.

His money was untouched. There was a new oilskin wallet containing the four hundred dollars left over from Hodge's advance, and a deerskin pouch with twenty dollars in change. Someone had tucked in a pack of forty cheroots and two boxes of lucifers.

He got dressed feeling guilty about leaving such nice folks. It was a long time since he'd met anyone like that.

When he got back to the kitchen, Lewis James was waiting with Sarah. He had a folded envelope in his hand.

'I got the feeling we couldn't talk you out of it,' he said, 'so I got you a ticket through to Cheyenne.'

'How much?' Jubal asked.

James shook his head. 'Forget it. Anyone who can walk out of the Bitterroots deserves a helping hand.'

Jubal shook theirs and walked down to the station. When he got there, he peeled two fifty-dollar bills off the wad and borrowed the stationmaster's pad to scribble a note.

It read: *Thanks. Maybe I'll see you again.*

He didn't think he would, but he felt indebted to the couple, so he sealed the note inside an envelope and gave a porter five dollars to deliver it.

Then the train pulled in and he climbed on board. Lewis James had booked him a sleeping berth through to Cheyenne, and he fell asleep while the big Baldwin engine was still spilling steam into the frosty air of Lewiston. By the time he woke again there was a porter knocking on his door and shouting that dinner was served.

Jubal climbed out of his bunk and splashed water over his face. It was cold. It woke him up better than the shouting. He checked his face and wondered if he ought to shave. He decided not: the faint growth of hair served to cover the claw marks down the left side of his face, where the cougar had ripped him. That felt like a long time ago. Much closer were the memories of his trek over the snow and the more immediate aches in his limbs.

For the first time since waking up in the James's cabin, he looked at his body. His left hand was puckered with the remnants of frostbite, the tips of the fingers withered and still discoloured. The right seemed more or less normal, though three fingers and the thumb were still red and shrunken in. His face was normal, apart from the marks of the mountain lion. And the rest of his body seemed recovered, if aching.

He pulled on a clean shirt and knotted a black tie under the collar. Then he pulled on his pants and buttoned the waistcoat

86

over his chest. Sarah James had done a good job on the suit: it looked spruce and almost new again.

He set the grey derby on his head and went out of the sleeping car into the corridor.

The dining car was two coaches down, but he could smell it long before and realized how hungry he was. He stepped inside and asked for a place on his own. There was one left, a whole table set farthest from the central stove in a corner where a window failed to shut properly. The draught made little difference to Jubal: he was used to the cold by now.

The meal tasted good. There was fresh river trout and steak to follow, with canned potatoes and sugared carrots and cabbage. Then apple pie with cream. And as much coffee as he wanted. When he was done eating, he ordered a brandy that he sipped slowly, knowing he shouldn't really drink it in his condition. He lit a cheroot and raised the blind from the window.

The draught swirled the smoke around, spilling it back in wavy lines that reminded him of the patterns on the Clearwater.

When he finished the thin tube of tobacco he crushed it out and dropped his money on the table.

The waiter saw that he had left considerably more than the usual tip and reminded Jubal as he opened the rearward door.

'I think you made a mistake, sir. You left too much.'

'Maybe,' grinned Jubal. 'But maybe I picked up more.'

He shoved the bills back into the Negro's hand and shut the door before the man could say anything else. The wind was blowing clear and cold off the snow, the sky flecked through with stars and the sparks of the smokestack. The locomotive blew a single long howl into the night. It echoed past the rumbling passenger cars and Jubal caught a moan of complaint from someone still inside the dining car. He grinned and turned away, feeling happy to be moving after ten Eyck.

Back inside the sleeper he stripped off his clothes and piled fresh coals on the fire. He banked the stove up high, so that it glowed and spat thin tongues of flame out through the grate. Luxuriating in the heat, he washed down and then climbed into the bunk.

87

He dragged all the available blankets over his body and then sank down inside.

There was something comforting about the rocking motion of the train, the steady drumming of the wheels, and even the whistle of the wind through the cracks in the wall. His berth was lit by the stove's glow and after a while he pushed the topmost blankets loose and shoved the sheets down clear of his torso. He touched the stock of the Spencer tucked under the last blanket alongside his body and glanced up at the Colt hung from the clothes hook beside the bunk.

'You left me cold, Jacob,' he murmured. 'I'll do you the same favour.'

Then he went to sleep.

CHAPTER ELEVEN

The same Negro who had served him at dinner woke him in the morning with a jug of hot water and one of coffee. He was beaming as he entered the berth.

'Mornin', suh, got you some good, hot coffee here. We'll be servin' breakfast in a few minutes. You like me to hold a table for you?'

'Thanks,' nodded Jubal, 'I'd appreciate that. I'd appreciate some information, too.'

'Whatever you want, suh. You just ask it.'

The over-large tip had done its work well.

'How many stops do we make before Cheyenne?' Jubal asked.

'About nine, suh. Not countin' the Granby halt.'

'Why not?' Jubal got suddenly worried. 'Why's that different?'

The porter chuckled. 'You was sound asleep, suh. Granby's where we hook up with the main line. We done that around midnight. You didn't miss nuthin', on account of there's nuthin' to miss. It's just a water halt. Why, old Mose – he runs the depot there, suh – he was complainin' that he hadn't seen no one since last week's train. No one ever goes to Granby, suh. Just through it.'

Jubal breathed a sigh of relief. 'How about the others?'

'Well, the next halt we make is at Baker, suh, which we is due to reach this afternoon. Then there's Caldwell. After that we make Nampa, then straight through to Pocatello.' The porter began to count the towns off on his fingers. 'There's Montpelier, Rock Springs, Rawlins, an' then Laramie. After that, it's Cheyenne, where you get off, suh.'

'How long?' Jubal asked. 'How long before we reach Cheyenne?'

'I can't make no promises, suh,' said the Negro, 'but if the snow holds off an' Mister Carver makes his usual time, we should be in Cheyenne inside the week.'

Jubal reached over to his coat and fumbled some coins out of the pocket. He counted off two fives and a big eagle.

'You be around when we reach those places?' he asked.

'Sure, suh.' The porter looked surprised. 'There might be folks comin' on board who'll need tendin' to. I'll be up an' waitin'.'

Jubal flipped a five through the air. The Negro caught it.

'You get any chance to talk to the stationhands?'

'Yessuh! I passes on news, an' they give me the same back.'

The second five spun across the room. 'You willing to ask some questions for me?'

'Yessuh!'

'Good.' The eagle joined the two fives in the Negro's pocket. 'There are three men I want to know about. If you hear of them getting off last week's train, I want to know. I want you to find me and hold the train until I get off. Can you do that?'

The man nodded enthusiastically and Jubal described Jacob ten Eyck, Greenhaugh and Schwatz. He hinted at more money for sound information and by the time the porter left his berth, he felt reasonably confident of learning if the outlaws had quit the earlier train along the line. He shaved and dressed, then went to get his breakfast.

He was still quite weak and decided that if he was to be in condition to take the three killers, he would need as much sleep as he could get. There was not much else to do, anyway. The train was small and sparsely passengered at this time of year. The sleeping car was located directly in front of the brake van, behind two empty carriages. Then there was the dining car, the tender and the locomotive itself. The complement of passengers was comprised of one elderly lady and her spinster daughter travelling eastwards to visit relatives in St Louis, two Army officers – a pair of captains – heading for Kansas City and a month's leave, two drummers returning from a trip west, and a trio of businessmen hoping to conclude a shipping deal between Seattle and New Orleans.

Jubal met them all and exchanged a few polite words as the

train rolled through the snowfields. Mostly he slept, rising from his bunk only when hunger dictated that he eat.

There was no word from the porter, and for three days Jubal remained quiet, almost permanently unconscious. The long rest did his resources of energy more good than he had dared hope, and on the fourth day he decided to stay awake after breakfast.

There was a poker school running in one of the passenger cars. The two women, one of the businessmen and the two officers were either asleep or talking in the second car. Jubal strolled past the table and saw the cards. One of the businessmen hailed him down.

'You interested in a game, friend?' He was a round-faced man with glowing cheeks and sparkling eyes. 'We could use an extra hand.'

'Depends,' said Jubal, tempted. 'What kind of stakes?'

'Ten cents a throw minimum. Top bet of twenty dollars.'

'Deal me in.'

He had been fascinated by the game for about as long as he could remember, and more than once had made a tidy killing through his natural skill with cards. Originally, poker had meant a way to pass the long, lonely evenings back in the Chicago orphanage, playing for matchsticks or scraps of paper against other kids with no money and too much time between dinner and sleep. He had a natural memory for the small details, and an instinctive understanding of the cards' running and his opponents' habits. Over the years those natural talents had been fined down to a keen appreciation that gave him a skill close to that of a professional. Also, he had the other thing in his favour: the indefinable thing called luck.

'What are we playing?' he asked, sitting down beside one of the drummers.

'Five card draw,' grunted the salesman. 'Aces high an' nothing wild.'

'Suits me.' Jubal eased a pile of change and a few notes on to the table. 'Name's Cade, by the way. Jubal Cade.'

'Glad to know you.' The man who had invited him to sit in spoke. 'I'm Ben Anstruther. This here's my partner, Lucas Drew. That's Martin Strother to your right, an' George Carson on the other side.'

Jubal murmured his greetings as he studied the players. Anstruther was holding the deal and most of the winnings. Lucas Drew was looking angry, which made his narrow face even uglier than was normal. Strother and Carson were looking cheerful, though why Carson should be happy about losing, Jubal didn't understand. Poker was a serious game to him, one he played to win. It could be fun only if the players were evenly matched and each one ready to try for the top. Losing was sometimes inevitable if the cards ran against a player, or if he was outclassed. But you didn't weep over it; or enjoy it.

Anstruther began to deal.

Jubal took a pair of eights, a seven, a three and a five. All except the five and the eight and the three in unmatched suits. He held the pair and the seven, changing the other cards for a deuce and a ten. Drew put down twenty cents. Carson stayed in. Jubal dropped out. Strother upped by ten. Anstruther matched him and forced Drew out of the hand. Carson went with him and Anstruther laid another twenty cents down. Strother saw him.

Anstruther was holding three queens and two deuces. He cleaned up a pot of change worth just over a dollar.

The next time round it was Drew who took the pot with a lucky flush.

Then Anstruther took another. After that, Strother won five dollars and Jubal picked up seventy cents.

Carson stayed unlucky, folding on three hands in succession before trying a wild bluff that almost cleaned him out when Jubal matched his two pair with a straight.

The drummer shrugged and grinned. 'I guess I'm better at selling than I am at cards,' he said. 'If you gents got no objections, I'll duck out.'

Jubal was glad to see him go: he didn't enjoy beating a bad player, and by now he had the others summed up.

Ben Anstruther was competent, no more. He used his money to force the hands and took too many wild chances, relying on bluff and massive raises to overwhelm his opponents. Lucas Drew was more cautious, almost too much so. Twice Jubal had watched him fold when he might have gone ahead and won. But his winnings were still mounting. Martin Strother was good. He was being careful with his stake, using it only when he was confident as he could be of taking the hand.

Jubal was about ten dollars up when Anstruther glanced at the ornate watch fobbed across his brocade vest.

'Eleven o'clock,' he said, snapping the hunter's lid closed. 'We can set a time to finish, or carry on regardless. How say you, gentlemen?'

'I like to eat,' said Drew. 'I paid for my food an' I want to eat it.'

Strother shrugged. 'I'll ride with the majority.'

Anstruther looked at Jubal: 'Mister Cade? How say you?'

'I get hungry, too,' grinned Jubal. 'Let's play to one. We can always come back.'

'So be it,' chortled Anstruther. 'You're to deal, I believe, Mister Cade.'

Jubal picked up the cards. They had agreed to shuffle on each fifth round or whenever someone dropped out. He riffled through the pack and passed it to Strother for cutting, then he flipped cards over the table.

Strother changed one; Anstruther, three. Drew called for two and Jubal followed suit. He took the hand for a dollar against Drew's pair of nines with two eights and two fours. Then Anstruther suggested they up the bidding. Lucas Drew looked disapproving and Strother looked a bit worried. Jubal agreed, and they settled on a minimum bet of fifty cents with a fifty dollar ceiling.

The change was simultaneously appealing and disadvantageous. Basically, it meant that the man with the most money could force anyone getting short out of the game. At the same time, it offered higher pots and the consequent inducement to play better.

Strother took the deal and handed Jubal the king and queen of Spades, the king of Diamonds, the ace of Clubs, and the six of Diamonds. Dealer dropped two. Drew asked for the same. Jubal took a long chance and dropped the queen and the six, taking the Diamond deuce and the six of Spades in return. Dealer changed one and looked happy. Anstruther folded, and Drew went with him. Jubal dropped fifty cents on the table. Strother grinned and raised by fifty. Jubal chose to sound the cards out and added a dollar to the pile in the centre. Strother got worried and paid to see him. Jubal set down his two kings. Strother folded and Jubal took the pot.

The next hand gave him two fours and two eights with a wild three in the middle. When it came time to change, he dropped the three and drew a useless nine. Drew had changed one, and so had Strother. Anstruther took two.

Drew put a dollar on the table. Jubal wondered about the low pairs for a moment and dumped his cards. Strother matched Drew's dollar and added three. Anstruther folded. Drew put three dollars down and then three more. Strother raised by five, and Drew got nervous. He paid to see. Strother laid a neat straight down: seven through jack; and took the pot.

It got back around to Jubal's turn. Strother took two, Anstruther the same. So did Drew. Jubal changed one. He already held two kings and a pair of deuces; he dropped a nine to fill the house with a third deuce.

Strother looked happy and folded two dollars on to the table. 'Now we're playing cards,' he smiled.

'Yeah,' said Anstruther, bouncing the pot up by five more dollars.

Lucas Drew said nothing. Just matched the stakes and waited for Jubal.

Jubal went along, preferring to let Strother and Anstruther waste their money while he waited to collect. The pot lifted in fives and tens. Drew folded. Jubal stayed with the game, still letting the others make the running. They reached the agreed maximum of fifty dollars and Anstruther grinned.

'I feel lucky,' he said. 'You gents feel like taking this on? What say we open the betting?'

Strother shrugged. 'Why not? Sky the limit?'

Jubal paused. His funds were held down to the two hundred and something he had in his pockets, plus the money on the table. He might need that much to find ten Eyck and claim the remainder of Hodge's promised reward.

But a full house was hard to beat. Especially with kings high. 'All right,' he said. 'Open the lid.'

'Raise by twenty,' smiled Anstruther. 'You going with me?'

'Yours and twenty more.' Jubal felt calm, suddenly confident of taking the money.

'And twenty,' said Strother. 'I hope you folks got good hands.'

Anstruther set more bills down, lifting the betting into the hundreds. Jubal matched him. Strother looked at his cards. He stayed in for two more rounds then shook his head.

'Jesus! I'm busted.'

'Luck of the cards,' grunted Anstruther. 'You coming with me, Cade?'

Jubal grinned and counted out three fifty-dollar bills. Anstruther looked surprised, then matched.

'See you.'

Jubal peeled two of the deuces on to the table. Anstruther set down two threes. Jubal added a third deuce. Anstruther set two sixes against the pair. Jubal put the two kings down and smiled as Anstruther grunted, 'Christ! I thought I had it that time.'

'Luck of the cards,' said Jubal. 'Just like you said.'

He reached his winnings in, calculating the amount. As best he could estimate, there was around six hundred and fifty dollars piled up on the table.

Anstruther laughed as he stood up. 'I reckon that now's a pretty good time to grab that meal they promised us.'

'Up to you, gentlemen,' said Jubal. 'I'm happy to give you a chance to take your money back.'

'Won and lost in fair play,' chuckled Anstruther. 'That was about the best damn' game I've had since I come west. I'd be happy to show my appreciation by havin' you join me for lunch.'

'Thanks,' said Jubal, 'I'd appreciate that.'

They went through to the dining car, where Anstruther introduced Jubal to his second partner.

Jonas Cardew obviously disapproved of his friends' interest in the fine art of poker. He looked up at Jubal over the edge of rimless spectacles and drew his narrow mouth down in a thin line that threatened to fade his grey moustache through the wrinkles of his chin.

'How much did you lose, Ben?' he asked.

'Few hundred,' grinned Anstruther. 'Jubal's one hell of a card player.'

'Cards and business seldom sit easily together,' said Cardew. 'Like wine and women.'

'Hell, Jonas,' shrugged Anstruther, 'we was just playing cards. No business involved.' He winked at Jubal. 'Nor any women to be had.'

Across the aisle of the car Mrs Stoneman and her daughter turned steely eyes in his direction.

'What is your business, Mister Cade?' Cardew asked. 'I don't believe you've ever mentioned that.'

'I'm a doctor,' said Jubal.

'Ah, doubtless heading east to start a practice.' Cardew nodded almost approvingly. 'Where do you plan to hang your shingle? Cheyenne? Or some place farther east?'

Jubal shook his head. 'I'm not planning to set up anywhere, just now. Fact is, I'm hunting three men.'

'Ah, you must be with the Government.' Cardew leaped eagerly to the wrong conclusion. 'What are they? Disease carriers? Something like that? I heard a rumour when we halted at Granby that some outpost had suffered a smallpox epidemic. Thank God it was in the mountains where the disease can't spread. Except to the Indians, of course; but that doesn't really count. I suppose you were checking that out?'

'Something like that,' grunted Jubal.

'Is there any danger here?' Drew got suddenly nervous. 'I mean, we couldn't catch it, could we?'

'No,' said Jubal quietly, 'I reckon it's all wiped out by now. No hope of any fresh outbreaks.'

'A curious way to put it,' said Cardew primly. 'Where are you reporting to?'

'Cheyenne,' said Jubal. 'I reckon they most likely got off there.'

'Don't we know some people in Cheyenne?' said Drew. 'Maybe they could help.'

Anstruther screwed up his round face. 'There's that factor,' he said slowly. 'Remember him? Used to ship us farm implements a year back. What was his name?'

Cardew pulled a thin notebook from his jacket. Flipping

through the pages, he said: 'Let's see. Cheyenne, ah ... C ... Nathan Toler, he was the one.'

'How about that other feller?' added Drew. 'Hammett? Dash Hammett, I think. The one was always reading cheap novels.'

'Ole Dash,' nodded Anstruther. 'He was the one. If anyone there'll know, it'll be him. He always did like to know what was going on.'

He reached over to snatch the notebook from Cardew's hands, then tugged a stub of pencil from his vest and began to scribble addresses on a blank sheet.

'Here, Jubal. I got 'em written down. Both addresses. We'll play one more hand, just you an' me.' He folded the paper and tucked it inside his vest. 'Your winnings against the names.'

'You're on,' said Jubal. 'But let's eat first.'

It was a good meal. Hot soup and then a plate of cold cuts, followed by roasted lamb out of the dining car's ice-box; cherry pie and coffee. Jubal shrugged off the brandy.

Afterwards they let the waiters clear the table and broke out a fresh pack of cards. Anstruther suggested a straight draw, but Jubal shook his head.

'No. That's too risky. We'll play three hands. Best player takes all.'

'Son,' grinned Anstruther, 'I like you. You could make a fine businessman. Cut the pack an' start dealing.'

Jubal dealt five cards to Anstruther, five more to himself.

Anstruther looked at his hand for a long time before changing two. Jubal stared at his own hand. He had three Hearts: the five, ten and seven. He also carried a ten of Spades and the six of Diamonds. The hand left him three alternatives. He could hold the pair and try for matching cards; keep the five, six and the seven in hope of making a straight; or try to fill the flush.

He opted for safety and held on to the pair.

He drew a third ten, a jack of Clubs and the queen of Hearts.

Anstruther put down two unmatched queens, a king, and then a nine and a ten. Jubal gathered up the pack and passed it across the table.

This time Jubal drew a near straight. He got the four of Diamonds, the five of Spades, the six of Hearts, and the seven of Diamonds. After that, the queen of Clubs. Filling the straight was tempting, but he decided it was too long a gamble. Instead, he dropped the first three cards and kept the seven and the queen. He got a deuce and two threes.

Anstruther let one card go. Then chuckled as he put two aces and two jacks down, with a loose four.

Jubal folded the used cards under the pack and dealt again.

When he picked them up he saw that he had two nines, one eight, a six and a five. Anstruther called for one. Jubal flipped it over and held his breath as he dropped three and hoped the wild odds turned out right.

It was a long chance that in any other game would have prompted him to fold and go with the pack. On the last turn it was all he could do. He held the pair along with his breath and hoped that luck was with him.

He turned his cards over.

Two nines. Diamonds and Spades.

Then a three of Clubs.

A six of Clubs.

Then another three: Hearts.

Anstruther shook his head and dropped a pair of eights down alongside an ace, a king and a jack.

'I know you're not cheatin' them,' he said, 'but I'd surely hate to play you for real.'

Jubal smiled and took the paper with the addresses on it.

'That was real,' he murmured. 'You don't know how much.'

When the train reached Cheyenne it was around midnight, Jubal had said his thanks and his goodbyes earlier that evening, so the only person who saw him leave the train was the Negro porter.

'Suh, I got word,' he called across the windswept platform. 'I just done talkin' with a couple o' friends. They said them fellers you was askin' about got off right here exactly one week since.'

Jubal set his baggage down and reached inside his coat. His hand came out with a coin cupped inside the fingers.

'Where'd they go?' he asked. 'You learn that?'

The Negro shook his head. 'They didn't go to no hotel, suh. All I could learn was they asked the way to the nearest stable.'

Jubal flipped the coin up in the air. It glinted in the station's lights.

'Where's that?'

'Be the Grandon place, suh.' The dark eyes followed the coin's trajectory. 'That's a block down from here. Due south. You can't hardly miss it, suh. Got a real big sign outside.'

'Thanks,' Jubal said. 'Here.'

He dropped the coin into the man's hand. It was a ten-dollar piece.

'Thank *you*, suh.'

Jubal watched the train pull out. The engineer let one blast of steam through the whistle mounted alongside the smokestack before the big wheels started turning and the whole caboose hauled clear of the Cheyenne depot. The rear lights faded away into the night, and from far off down the tracks he heard one last, lonesome scream as he humped his gear down the empty streets.

The Grandon Stable was closed up for the night, but there was a dingy-looking hotel facing the barn. Jubal booked himself into a single room. The place was called the Union Palace, and looked like the kind of hotel people too tired to wander any farther might use. The foyer was lit dim, the carpet worn threadbare by tired boots. The plush chairs were stained with ash and spilled drinks, shiny from long usage. The desk was much the same: once it had been handsome, veneered and polished. Now the polish was gone and the veneer was scratched by striking matches and dropped baggage. There was a pot plant at one side that looked like it was dying for want of a drink, or maybe on account of the atmosphere. The vestibule smelled of stale smoke and sweat and whiskey.

So did the clerk Jubal woke.

He had been handsome once. A long time ago, before he gave up and started drinking too much. His black hair was slicked back with an excess of grease that failed to hide the bald patch and his eyes held the tell-tale veins of bottle-love. His breath proved the point, and when he came up off his couch behind the desk Jubal stepped back a pace from the sour whiskey fumes.

'Yeah? Watcha want?'

Jubal was tired, not in any mood to accept hostility from a man paid to do a job.

'Guess,' he said coldly. 'What you selling?'

99

'A joker.' The clerk flexed his shoulders and let one hand drop under the counter. 'You want a room, or not?'

'For the night,' said Jubal. 'I'll want a bath in the morning. When can I take it?'

'We got hot water from six on,' grunted the clerk. 'You want a call then?'

'When's the stable open?'

'Six. Same as us, on account of we own it.'

Jubal glanced at the register the clerk had automatically thrust in front of him. There were nine entries for the past week and a half. None of them looked anything like ten Eyck or Greenhaugh or Schwatz. He described the outlaws to the clerk. The man shook his head.

'I ain't seen no one like that.'

'All right,' Jubal said. 'Wake me at six.'

'Jesus! That means I got to do it,' whined the clerk. 'Can't you leave it a bit?'

Jubal shook his head.

'What's with you?' the man called after him as he headed for his room. 'You some kinda early bird?'

Jubal nodded. 'The kind that worries worms.'

CHAPTER TWELVE

The knocking woke him in the morning and he rolled out of the bed with a quick glance at the half hunter on the table alongside. It was five minutes after six. The clerk was outside his door with a towel and a sour expresion.

'Bath is down the end. There should be soap inside.'

There was. A thick lump of gritty stuff that rasped against his skin as he scrubbed himself clean. The tub was dirty, with a grey ring around the inner sides, but the water was hot and the soap helped to wake him up. There was a big jug of cold water that he used to sluice the soap off, and a separate bowl of hot water for shaving.

Jubal got cleaned up and dressed fast. Then he left his gear with the day clerk and went over to the stable. There was an old man chewing on a pipe as he swept out the stalls.

He seemed surprised to find anyone coming in so early and canted his broom against his shoulder like a trooper coming to attention.

'You sell horses?' Jubal asked.

'Sure do, sir!' The oldster grinned. 'We got some nice stock in, just now. You just take a look at that black there. Stall's just down from the door. Part quarter horse, that one. Touch of mustang fer stayin' power. Gelding, it is. Handles like a dream come true.'

'I don't want to buy,' grinned Jubal. 'At least, not yet.'

'Well, we got a few stalls spare,' said the old man. He sounded disappointed. 'Cost you a dollar a day fer all found.'

'I don't have a pony, either,' said Jubal. 'I just want to ask a few questions.'

'I ain't too good at answerin' them.' The broom came down and slumped on the dirty straw. 'My job's horses, not questionings.'

A dollar glinted in Jubal's hand, lifting from palm to palm.

The oldster's eyes followed the movement like a prairie hawk watching a gopher.

'O' course it depends on the ones asked.'

'You sell any horses lately?' Jubal asked.

'A few.' The eyes were fixed on the spinning coin. 'Round five in the last week.'

Jubal tossed the coin over. The old man caught it with more energy than he put into his sweeping.

'Tell me about them,' said Jubal. 'There could be another dollar for the right answer.'

'Well.' The oldster scratched his head. 'Was a cowhand come by yesterday an' bought a nice little mustang someone left in payment o' debts. Sweet little piebald mustang with a nice temperament fer a range pony. Then there was Mort Kane bought a plough horse coupla weeks ago. An' three fellers come in together wantin' fast horses. Bought my best stock an' give me top prices, too.'

'What'd they look like?' Jubal interrupted.

'Well, one was a big chestnut. Part Arab an' part Morgan. Had a purty little blaze down his nose. Fast runner, too . . .'

'The men!' Jubal rasped. 'What did they look like?'

'Hell, sonny, don't get impatient. I'll come to that. They bought a black outta Hank Janson's stock. An' that's good. Got speed an' guts, 'ceptin' Hank's horses got a tendency to go lame. Never could figger out why that should be, but it happens. Third was a skewball. Now that had . . .'

A second dollar spun through the pungent air.

'The men who bought them,' Jubal repeated. 'Tell me about them.'

'Damn' youngsters,' grumbled the stablehand. 'Ain't never the time to say "howdo". Allus on the move to hither an' yon, an' scarce the time to say "goo'bye", neither.'

He bit the dollar and tucked it away with the first.

'Well, the first feller was a big man. Dark hair an' a big black beard. He had real cold eyes. Grey an' mean like a coldwater stream in Winter. There was another 'bout half his size. Ugly little guy with sneaky looks and stringy hair. Fair, he was. I never took to him. Never did take to a man as favours a scattergun. Third one was kinda quiet. Tall an' skinny, he was. Had a beard like the first, but not much hair on top.'

'You know where they went?' asked Jubal. 'They say anything about that?'

'Nope. Just settled their bill in nice new coin an' took their horses. Bought tack, too. Three saddles an' all the rest.'

'Thanks.' Jubal wondered if the gang was already clear of Cheyenne. 'You're real helpful.'

'Pleasure,' grinned the oldster, showing off a set of blackened teeth. 'There ain't too many youngsters care to talk a spell.'

'I guess not,' said Jubal. 'But I'm not surprised, either.'

He went back to the hotel and ordered breakfast. It was seven o'clock and the sun was barely up through a thick bank of grey cloud. After eating he got directions to the offices of Nathan Toler and Dash Hammett. He collected his gear and set off down the street. If he had to stay in Cheyenne over any length of time, he preferred to stay some place better than the Union Palace.

Cheyenne was a big place. Bigger than any he had seen over the past few months, and at first the size and the noise was disturbing.

The town was located at the end of the old Goodnight-Loving cattle trail, a way-station on the pioneer route to California. Cows and railroads went mostly together, though since the Kansas Pacific had pushed the tracks out from St Louis through Denver, the latter town had taken most of the trade. Even so, with the Union Pacific joining the KP there, Cheyenne was wide-open and booming.

Vast areas of land were taken up by cattle pens that spread out from the rail depot. There were side-tracks and shunting yards flanked by barns and warehouses and grubby offices. If there was a residential section, it was hidden away from the stockyards and the tracks behind a wall of saloons and stores and whorehouses. The streets were set out on a grid pattern, wide avenues of packed dirt linking at right-angles with secondary streets. There were cowboys and carriages jostling for position in the roads, and the sidewalks were packed with townsfolk and transients.

Nathan Toler's office was situated mid-way down one of the central roads.

It was on the second floor of a three-storey building with a false-front that added two extra levels of space to make an impressive frontage. The street level was taken up by a cattle buyer's office. Toler's was reached from a central stairwell that opened on to a fusty balcony. The office had a brass plate on the door that read *N. Toler, Factor*.

Jubal knocked and went inside.

A grey-haired woman in a severe black dress looked at him from over the top of steel half-spectacles.

'Yes?' Her voice was as unwelcoming as her eyes. They both matched the colour of her hair.

'Ben Anstruther sent me,' smiled Jubal. 'Ma'am.'

He dropped his gear and took off his hat. The woman let some of the ice go out of her look at seeing his politeness.

'Mr Anstruther? Why yes, that nice man from Oregon. But we haven't dealt with him in two years. What could he want now?'

Jubal smiled some more. 'I got a message for Mr Toler, ma'am. Ben took the train on through to the East, but he told me specially to come see Mr Toler.'

'Well,' said the woman, 'he's awfully busy just now. I'm not sure if he has time.'

There was dust on the filing cabinet behind her desk and the carpet was losing its colour under the weight of the years. Jubal glanced down: the area leading to the inner office was untrodden, dust gathering outside the door. He looked straight at the woman and smiled again.

'It won't take a moment, ma'am. And it does mean a lot.' He omitted to add '*To me.*'

'All right.' She came close to simpering. 'Go on in.'

Nathan Toler was very much like Cardew. He looked as though he had been pinched into his suit and the fit hurt him. Sallow wattles hung over the stiff collar and a faint odour of mustiness and brandy hung around his office.

He took unkindly to Jubal's request for help.

'Why should I?' he asked in a dry voice. 'I've not worked with Anstruther in years. He deals mostly with Hammett now.'

Jubal shrugged. 'Things change. I was talking to Ben just yesterday. He told me specially to look you up because he didn't have time.'

'You mean he wants to use me again?' demanded Toler.

'Possibly,' Jubal lied. 'He's headed for New Orleans, but he'll be coming back this way. If the deal gets fixed there could be plenty of work in it.'

So far as he knew, Anstruther's deal was to ship goods up the coast to Oregon, but if Toler could help him find the ten Eyck gang he wasn't overly concerned with the niceties of business ethics.

'Well, in that case.' Toler scratched his nose. 'If it does mean more business.'

Jubal nodded vigorously.

'I'd ask around the Red Dog or the Lazy Cow,' said Toler, looking disapproving. 'They seem to be the favourite haunts of the riff-raff.'

'Thanks,' said Jubal, standing up. 'I'm grateful.'

'I hope Ben is, too,' hawked Toler. 'In tangible ways.'

Jubal ducked out before he got asked any awkward questions and went to find Hammett.

The second office was brighter than Toler's, with a prettier secretary and a lot less dust on the files. But Hammett wasn't there.

'He'll be in the Dollar Queen, I imagine,' said the girl in answer to Jubal's smile. 'He mostly goes there for a drink at this time of day.'

She gave him directions to the saloon and a decent hotel. It was still too early to eat, so Jubal booked a room in the Albion Hotel and left his gear there.

The Dollar Queen was a block down, with a big, gold-painted sign hung outside in the shape of a coin. It was a rich-looking place. The boards of the floor were polished and there were potted plants dotted around the interior. A bouncer was settled on a stool just inside the glass doors, and Jubal spotted two more spaced out down the long central room. There was a stairway leading up to the first storey with another bouncer guarding the head, where the balcony led off to a series of closed rooms.

Down one side of the main room there was a mahogany-fronted bar with a marble top. Beer taps were set against the marble and about seven barkeeps were busy pulling glasses of foaming ale or pouring whiskey for a mob of customers. There were card tables set up with five games going, and a roulette wheel clicking at the far end. Two faro tables were in operation, and a big wheel o' fortune was spinning brightly midway along.

Jubal went up to the bar.

He ordered whiskey and asked for Hammett. The barkeep pointed to a table across the room, set back inside an alcove near the stairs.

'You'll find him there, friend. Most like he'll be with Liliane.'

Jubal picked up his drink and went over to the alcove. Behind the plant shading it off from the saloon, there was a tall, grey-haired man in deep conversation with a blonde girl in a blue dress cut low enough to spark ideas without revealing their source.

Hammett looked up as Jubal's body shut off the light.

'You lost, mister?'

'No.' Jubal shook his head and grinned. 'I'm looking for Dash Hammett. Ben Anstruther told me to look him up.'

'Ben?' Hammett sounded pleased to hear the name. 'What's that old buzzard want?'

'Not him; me,' Jubal said. 'Ben lost a poker game and gave me your address. Said you could help me.'

'Sit down.' Hammett ushered Jubal into the alcove, tugging the blonde girl closer against him to make room. 'Any friend of Ben's is one of mine. You got a drink?'

Jubal showed his glass and Hammett grinned, topping it up. He filled his own and the girl's.

'This is Liliane. Sweetest thing this side of Washington. What did Ben say I could do for you?'

Jubal explained. He left out the reward and the business at Hope. Smallpox was the kind of subject that scared people off; the reward was something he didn't plan to share or give away. He made it sound like he was hunting the outlaws on behalf of Anstruther.

106

'Hell,' said Hammett, 'they could be any place here. Folks in Cheyenne don't ask too many questions about a man's money. So long as he's got coin in his pocket he's an all right feller.'

Jubal sipped his drink, wondering if Anstruther's help was worth the risking of his stake.

'Tell you what,' said Hammett after a while, 'Toler could be right about the Red Dog or the Lazy Cow, but there's a whole passel of saloons where these fellers might hang out. I know some people as wouldn't mind asking around, so I'll put the word out. Where you staying?'

'The Albion,' said Jubal. 'Just up the block from your office.'

'I know it,' said Hammett. 'Big rooms with rotten food. Meet me back here tomorrow. I'll buy you a drink and tell what I found out.'

He turned back to Liliane and whispered something to her. Jubal took the hint and left.

He went back to the Albion and learned that Hammett was right about the food. His room was good. The bed was soft and the whole place was heated against the Winter cold, but the food was awful.

That night he ate out and spent some time hanging round the central saloons, hoping to spot one of the gang. He gave up around midnight and went back to sleep. In the morning he took breakfast – which was as bad as the evening meal – and then killed time until noon.

Hammett was in the Dollar Queen with Liliane scooped up on his knees. The factor was about three-quarters drunk, but he still recognized Jubal.

'Men you want been seen in three places,' he slurred. 'Sounds like they got their horses in a stable on the south side. Willy's Livery, it's called. Stands close to the Red Dog, which is the second place. The other is a whorehouse run by a lady known as Annabelle York. Red Anny they call her, on account of the way her clients look after they come out.'

Liliane shushed him with her fan and told him to watch his mouth.

Jubal thanked him.

'Weren't nothing,' grinned Hammett. 'I'd come down there with you, only I got more important business right here.'

He shoved a hand up against Liliane's cleavage as she squealed protests. Whether against his hand, or what he'd said, Jubal didn't wait to find out.

He went back to the Albion and locked his door. Then he broke the Spencer down and cleaned the parts. After that he checked the Colt over. When he was satisfied that both guns were working as best they could he loaded them and waited for nightfall.

He ate in a restaurant set down a side street. It was quiet and clean, and the food was good. He accepted an extra helping of apple pie with cream and smiled as he settled his bill.

'Come on back,' said the fat lady who ran the place and liked to see healthy men eat her cooking. 'I'd be happy to see your friends.'

'I doubt it,' grinned Jubal. 'They're not friends, and they'd most likely turn your cream sour.'

CHAPTER THIRTEEN

Annabelle's was a double-storey building built up like a Georgia mansion house. It had a long, low porch with red lanterns hanging all along the frontage and horses tied to the hitching-rails all along the porch. The windows were made of coloured glass, so that the street outside was sparkled with light like a child's kaleidoscope. Above the porch there was a recessed balcony where those girls not 'entertaining' called invitations to the passers-by.

Jubal headed for the main door, where a thickset Negro stood guard.

'Evenin', suh. Welcome to Madame Annabelle's.' His eyes checked Jubal with professional skill. 'Go right on in, suh, you'll find a drink waitin'.'

He was right. Inside the door the place opened out into a large room with a bar set off in one corner. There was a tiny vestibule manned by a short Negro who took Jubal's hat and passed him a wooden token.

'That's for yore first drink, suh. I'll have yore derby waitin' when you're ready to leave. Have fun.'

The bar was built off from the vestibule, faced by the main part of the room. There was a thick red carpet on the floor and tables and chairs spread around the sides. At the far end was a dais with a Victrola mounted like an altar. Dried flowers flanked the machine and its tinny notes accompanied the random movements of the dancers wavering between the tables. The male half of each couple seemed to be mostly dressed, at least partially. The female was mostly in garters and stays.

There was a cloying, sweet scent in the air that Jubal found hard to place.

He went up to the bar and showed his token.

'What'll it be, sir?' The bartender was white. From skin to shoes. He wore a white shirt with a floppy white tie, white trousers and white, lace-up boots. His skin was white, as though

109

109

it hadn't seen sunshine in a long time, and when he smiled his teeth were white, too. Only his hair was different: black.

'Whiskey,' Jubal said.

It was good whiskey. Better than the saloons served. Jubal sipped it slowly, savouring the taste. It sat easy on his belly, sliding down like honeyed fire. He hooked his elbows on the bar and studied the room.

The girls came from a multiplicity of races. There were tall Scandinavians and dark, flashing-eyed women from Mexico or Spain; Chinese girls with slanted eyes and blue-black hair hanging long down their naked backs; Indian women and lithe, sway-hipped Negresses; more of races he couldn't recognize. Some were dancing, others lounged around the tables, or sat on the banquettes flanking the walls.

'Take your time,' said a soft voice from his left in a cultured accent, 'I run the best house this side of St Louis, so I expect a man to be choosey.'

Jubal turned and found his eyes looking at a short, plump woman with a face that had once been beautiful and was now still handsome.

'Ma'am?' he said. 'You'd be Annabelle, I guess.'

'That's me.' She pirouetted and curtsied. 'Annabelle York. Welcome to my establishment.'

Jubal grinned. Annabelle was pushing fifty, but acted like a girl playing the dowager. She was fat, bound in with whale-bone, and when he looked at her face more closely, he saw it was lined under the powder. There was a dark mole sprouting hair on her left cheek. But he liked her.

'What can I suggest?' She folded her fan and set her hands together. There was no sound of a clap, but the girls un-occupied with clients stood up just the same. 'Why not take your pick while you finish your drink? Don't take too long: my girls are in demand.'

Jubal emptied his glass and put it down on the bar.

'Ma'am,' he said, 'I'm not looking for a girl. I want to find a man.'

He got no farther because Annabelle did clap her hands. It brought a Colt's Peacemaker out from under the bar. Held and cocked in the grasp of the white-clad barkeep.

'I do not run that kind of house,' said Annabelle. 'If your tastes go that way, I suggest you find some other establishment.'

Jubal looked at the Colt. It was very still, aimed firm on his chest.

'You got me wrong, ma'am.' He set his hands down on the bar where the keeper could see them. 'There's three men I've been looking for. I heard they used your place.'

'I don't care.' Annabelle's face lost most of its faded glory and got ugly. 'Anyone who comes here is a guest. We ask no questions and expect a few lies. In here, a man is as good as his money. We don't expect people to come in making trouble.'

'I'm not making any trouble,' grated Jubal. 'Just asking if you know anyone called Jacob ten Eyck.'

Annabelle's blackened lashes flickered and the rouge on her cheeks went pale.

'He'd be with two other men,' said Jubal. 'A little blond guy called Jimmy Schwatz, and a skinny man called Jeb Greenhaugh.'

Annabelle's movement was instinctive, almost hidden. But Jubal still caught the upward flick of her lashes, as though she wondered if someone in the rooms above was listening. She shook her head, then glanced at the barkeep.

'Escort this person out, Matthew. See him on his way.'

The barkeep came out from behind the counter with the Colt still levelled on Jubal's chest.

'Look, I don't want to make trouble.' Jubal backed away from the gun. 'I just wanted to find them. They killed a lot of people.'

'Not here,' said Annabelle. 'And here is all I care about. See him out, Matthew.'

The white-clad barkeep nodded instinctively.

As he ducked his head, Jubal danced sideways and swung his left foot up in a short, vicious arc. His toe hit the man hard on the right knee. At the same time Jubal powered to the right, landing on the carpet.

The barkeep screamed as his kneecap shattered and fired his pistol into the door.

Jubal rolled, hauling the Colt clear of the holster. The

barkeep fell over and slumped against the rail. He lifted his gun, firing blind into the room. Someone screamed. Jubal shot him once.

The bullet hit midway down his ribs. It blew his heart into ragged pieces and went on through the veneer of the bar. There was the sound of breaking glass. The white shirt got suddenly bloody and the man called Matthew opened his mouth and spat blood over his legs and Annabelle's carpet. Jubal twisted, sensing rather than hearing, the sound of the outer door swinging open as the black doorman came through.

He was holding a carved billystick in his right hand, and when he saw Jubal, he headed straight across the carpet.

Jubal shouted at him 'Don't!'

The Negro kept on coming, his club lifted high in readiness for a strike.

Jubal shot him in the leg. He aimed the bullet at the lower bones, the tibia and fibula, so as to cripple the Negro without killing him.

The doorman went down like a felled tree. The club was still clutched in his hand, but his leg was broken so that he could only crawl towards Jubal, dragging his twisted leg behind like a bloody anchor.

Jubal stood up.

The dancers were cowered down around the walls and Annabelle was staring wide-eyed at the corpse on the floor, at Jubal, and at the groaning Negro.

Jubal shoved his gun up against her ample breasts, twisting the barrel into her flesh.

'Who's up there?' he snarled. 'How many of them?'

She shook her head, and mumbled something that might have been pain or hate or refusal. It didn't matter, because Jimmy Schwatz shouted from the head of the staircase and fired his scattergun. Jubal couldn't hear the words enough to remember them, but he thought the blond outlaw said '*Goddam you Cade, I knew we shoulda killed you.*' After that it all got blocked out behind the roar of the Meteor and Jubal was powering away from the bar in an attempt to avoid the flying shot.

He felt pellets hit his legs and doubled over into a ball,

rolling behind the cover of a table as the room filled up with screams and the stink of black powder smoke. Annabelle took the bulk of the outlaw's fire. The ought-ought gauge shot tore her face away down to the bone. It ripped her dress apart so that one pendulous breast flopped loose and hung in bloody tatters over the stained remnants of her gown. Her fat body lifted sideways under the weight of the pellets, spilling a stinking flood of urine on to the carpet. She came to rest on the sprawled body of her barkeep, her face bleeding into his groin.

Jubal came up on his knees. He hurled the table across the room and powered after it, diving for the foot of the stairs.

Schwatz was gone, and Jubal remembered that he carried a single-barrel shotgun.

He lifted up on his feet and ran towards the head.

Schwatz came out of his room with a Remington Army in his hand and the shotgun in his left. Jubal hit the head and powered sideways, angling for the closest door. More pellets splattered the woodwork and a woman screamed as her client fumbled into his pants.

'Sorry,' grunted Jubal, 'but there's some rough trade in to-night.'

He bellied down on the plushy carpet and angled the Colt out through the door.

Three shots splintered the wood above his head. He fired once. Blind. There was the sound of running feet.

He triggered three more shots blind down the balcony then reloaded.

There was the sound of a door opening and a high-pitched scream. A louder cry. One shot. Then silence.

Jubal went out on to the balcony in a low dive that fetched him up against the rail. People were screaming below and Annabelle's clients were fighting to get clear of the bordello. From down the balcony came a steady, high-toned wail. It came from behind a swinging door.

Jubal stood up and ran towards it.

Inside the room a girl in high-heeled shoes and black, suspender-fastened stockings was crouched down against a blood-stained bed. The sheets were crimson, their coloration stemming in heavy spurts from the chest of the man sprawled back against the pillows.

His torso was covered with blood, most of it pumping out from the hole over his heart. More came from his face, where Jimmy Schwatz's scattergun still rested, embedded in the fractured bone, between the mouth and the eyes.

The man was wearing high-buttoned boots, the kind whores wear, and the bullet hole in his chest was pumping through a black whalebone corset. Blood-spattered curtains fluttered behind the bed, where the window was open on to the street below.

Jubal went past the wailing girl and looked down.

A bullet cut chips from the frame beside his face.

He fired back at the muzzle flash then went out through the window in a rolling dive that bounced him off the rear porch and slid him on to the dark alley below. He landed on his feet and tumbled sideways. The shock jarred him enough that he fell down and winced.

Until another shot blasted from out of the darkness.

Behind Annabelle's place the ground was taken up with low shacks and stockyards. Some were occupied, because he could hear cows lowing nervously at the sounds of gunfire. He huddled behind a fencepost, waiting for feeling to come back into his legs as he listened to the cattle bellowing and estimated Jimmy Schwatz's path.

It wasn't too hard to follow. The outlaw was panicked and running. Instead of heading back into town, he was moving out, working his way through the yards north of Cheyenne towards the open country beyond.

Jubal stood up and ran for the alley flanking the whorehouse.

He powered across the entrance, where his body would show up against the lights.

A shot echoed from the darkness of the stockyards.

Jubal ran for the nearest fence.

He ducked under the rails and went across the empty pen. On the far side he saw rails gleaming in the pale light of the moon. He tapped his gun against the metal. A shot answered the sound from his right. He moved that way.

The tracks were laid straight through the yards, or the yards built around the tracks. Either way, Jimmy Schwatz was hiding amongst the pens.

Or running, more like.

Jubal drifted over, cat-footing past the empty fences until he reckoned he was close to the outlaw.

Then he shouted.

'You're running, Jimmy! Where you going?'

A bullet whistled over his head.

'You missed, Jimmy! What's the trouble? Can't you work without a scattergun?'

Another shot blazed out.

'That's six, Jimmy,' shouted Jubal. And stood up.

Twelve feet ahead he saw a white undershirt lift into view.

'Don't kill me! Fer Christ's sake, please don't kill me.'

Schwatz had both his hands lifted up high in the air. Neither one was carrying a gun. Jubal levelled his Colt on the man's chest, wondering. He thought about all the dead people in Kempton and the others back in Hope. All the ones who died when Jimmy Schwatz triggered his scattergun. He thought about the dead man in Annabelle's brothel. And the way Schwatz had wanted to kill him back along the river.

'Why not?' he asked. 'Tell me why not.'

'Fer Chrissakes! You're a doctor, ain't you?'

'Sure,' said Jubal, moving forwards. 'I'm a doctor, and doctors kill diseases. You're a disease, Jimmy. Like smallpox or any other dirty contagion that kills off decent folks without thinking about it. Why shouldn't I kill you same as killing them?'

'Oh my God!' Schwatz moaned. 'I ain't got no gun. I'm unarmed! You can't just shoot me down.'

'You did,' rasped Jubal. 'You killed people everywhere you been. You killed in Kempton and Hope. You shot folks there with no reason. I got a reason. Tell me why not.'

Schwatz sucked in great heavy breaths that defined his position even better than the faint glimmer of his undershirt.

'You can't,' he said.

'I can,' Jubal grated. 'I really can.'

And squeezed the trigger.

The first bullet hit Jimmy Schwatz just above his belt. It

ruptured his stomach and went out through his rear ribs. He doubled over so that the second hit his chest and tore through his right lung. He curled up in a tight ball, spitting blood into the moon's light. The third caught his left shoulder and spun him round with the broken arm flying loose from the hole in his belly. The one that hurt the most.

He landed on his back and tried to scream. It was difficult, because his mouth kept filling up with blood and it was getting hard to breathe. Instead of a scream he made a choking, grunting sound, like a pig snuffling in the dirt. From where he lay he could see Jubal walking towards him, his right hand thrust out. The moon emerged from behind the cloud and the gun in Jubal's hand glistened briefly in the light. Schwatz moaned and rolled over.

The full impact of Jubal's bullets was not yet realized; shock had numbed the killer's nerves so that he still thought he might have a chance. Painfully, he began to crawl towards his own gun.

Jubal seemed to be moving with a dreadful slowness, almost as though he was playing with Schwatz. Jimmy got to the Remington and fumbled the loading gate open. It was hard ejecting the spent shells, because his left hand was slick with blood and he could barely close his fingers on the pistol. He wished he had kept his scattergun. He dragged a handful of cartridges from his pants' pocket and mumbled a curse as most of them fell to the ground. He thumbed one into the cylinder and glanced back over his shoulder.

Jubal was standing silent, waiting.

'Go ahead, Jimmy. See if you can do it. I'll give you a chance.'

Schwatz gasped as he saw Jubal's face. It was an ugly mask of pure hatred. Jubal's eyes blazed as though lit by some inner fire, and his mouth was thinned out to a tight, vengeful line. His nostrils flared as if scenting death and across his cheekbones, the skin was drawn taut, glistening white in the moonlight.

Schwatz moaned, shaking his head. It had never really occurred to him that one day he might be shot down in cold blood. That was something reserved for *his* victims. Now he knew with horrible certainty that it was happening to him.

116

'Go on. Try it.' Jubal's voice was harsh, rasping from between narrowed lips. 'Try it, Jimmy.'

Schwatz coughed up a thick gobbet of blood and snapped the loading gate closed. He got his legs doubled under him and thrust out, hurling his bleeding body forwards as he twisted round, triggering the Remington.

Jubal fired in the same instant.

Schwatz's bullet cut air two inches from his face. His own hit the outlaw under the chin. It went in through his lower jaw and tore on through the roof of his mouth. Entering the cranium, it pulped Schwatz's brain and exploded out through the top of his skull. There was a flash of white bone and fluttering blond hair, then a dark gout of blood that shone black in the pale light. Schwatz's head jerked backwards so that his eyes stared up, sightless, at the sky. Jubal fired again, smashing Schwatz's face into raw, crimson pulp.

The outlaw twitched, his spine arcing so that for a moment he was bowed, weight resting on heels and head. Then he made a dull, gargling noise and his body collapsed, still.

Jubal stared at the corpse, feeling the rage drain slowly from his body. He levered the spent shells clear of the Colt and reloaded. The falling cases made tiny plopping sounds as they dropped into the spreading pool of blood still pulsing from Schwatz's stomach and chest and head.

'I'll send you company,' he murmured. 'Soon.'

He turned away and began to walk back towards the brothel. There was a crowd gathered outside and two deputies were on guard at the door, holding Winchesters like a barrier against the curious onlookers.

Jubal pushed through and climbed on to the porch.

'Sorry, mister,' grunted the nearest lawman. 'No one's allowed in.'

A girl shouted from behind the deputy and a thickset man with a grizzle of grey beard stubble on his face and a tarnished star on his shirt stepped out through the door.

'Let him by, Hank. I want to talk with this one.'

Jubal went inside. The bodies of Annabelle and Matthew were still stretched out by the bar, and at the far end of the big room the girls and some of the men were huddled together like nervous sheep.

'Name's Dupree,' said the marshal. 'I'm the law around Cheyenne. Seems you had a hand in this.'

Jubal nodded.

'Way I heard the story, it was you killed Matthew,' said Dupree calmly. 'Seems you shot him an' then wounded Jonas. After that it gets kinda confused. Want to tell your side?'

'Matthew drew on me,' said Jubal. 'He was holding a gun when I drew.'

'That right?' Dupree turned to the crowd. 'Any o' you see it?'

A man stepped forwards. 'Matthew had a gun on him, right enough, Bill. I don't fer sure know what the little feller did because he moved so goddam fast. But one moment Matthew was holdin' on him an' the next he was down an' dead.'

'What about Jonas?' asked Dupree.

'He was coming at me with a club,' grunted Jubal. 'I shot him in the leg. I had no reason to kill him.'

Dupree looked at the Negro, who shrugged and nodded.

'So.' The lawman stared at Jubal with a speculative look in his calm blue eyes. 'That just leaves Annabelle an' the feller upstairs. An' the man as used the scattergun on them.'

'He was an outlaw called Jimmy Schwatz,' said Jubal. 'He's out in the stockyards. I shot him.'

'Hell, mister,' grunted Dupree, 'you shore had yourself a wild time. What are you? A hired gun?'

'I'm a doctor,' murmured Jubal wryly.

'Hell!' Dupree looked surprised for the first time. 'What you tryin' to do? Build up a practice?'

CHAPTER FOURTEEN

Dupree had Jubal wait while he questioned Annabelle's girls and those clients willing to admit to seeing the gunfight.

It put Jubal in a difficult position, because he was concerned that word might filter back to ten Eyck and give the outlaw a chance to escape. At the same time, he could not leave the whorehouse without coming under the guns of the marshal and his deputies. Nor did he want to reveal his full purpose for fear that Dupree might arrest ten Eyck and Greenhaugh to hold against the killings in Montana. On balance it seemed best to wait. And hope that he could still find the outlaws when Dupree let him go.

The deputy called Hank and another called Wilbur were despatched to find Schwatz's body and bring it in.

When they returned, Wilbur was looking queasy and there were stains on his shirtfront. Hank, too, looked green. Dupree asked them what was wrong.

Wilbur helped himself to a healthy slug of whiskey, shaking his head as though in disbelief.

'Jesus! I ain't never seen a man shot up like that,' he groaned. 'He was damn' near blowed apart.'

Dupree lifted the blanket covering the corpse. He stared at it for a long time, then turned to Jubal.

'You hafta do that to him? Wasn't one bullet enough?'

'No.' Jubal shook his head. 'No, it wasn't. There's a lot of people in Montana dead on account of Schwatz. I paid him back in kind.'

Dupree looked suspicious. 'You a bounty hunter? I ain't overly fond o' bounty killers.'

'Like I told you,' murmured Jubal, 'I'm a doctor. This was personal.'

'Hell!' Dupree shook his head. 'Some kinda doctor.' He turned to Hank. 'He have a gun on him?'

'In his hand,' nodded the deputy. 'There was two shots in the chambers. Been fired recently, too. It looked to me like it happened the way Cade told us.'

'Yeah,' said the marshal, slowly. 'Folks here say the same. I guess the doc's in the clear.'

'Does that mean I can go?' Jubal asked.

'I reckon,' grunted Dupree. 'It don't seem there's anything to hold you on.'

Jubal stood up. The lawman motioned for him to wait. He came over from the body and stood looking down at Jubal.

'I run a clean town, Cade,' he said carefully, pitching his voice too low for anyone else to hear, 'and I aim to keep it that way. If you've got a quarrel with anyone else, don't have it in my town. In fact, it'd be a whole lot better if you rode on. Annabelle an' Matthew had friends who might just decide to forget the law an' come after you. Be best if you quit Cheyenne.'

'I'll bear that in mind,' Jubal nodded. 'I wasn't aiming to stay long, anyway.'

'Good,' said Dupree, turning away. 'That's good.'

It was past midnight, and Cheyenne was beginning to shut down for the night. The lights were going out in the saloons and the streets were mostly empty. The moon was hidden behind thick cloud and a cold wind was blowing through the darkened buildings. Jubal shivered, turning up the collar of his jacket. He settled the grey derby firmly over his dark hair and made his way to the Red Dog.

He spotted Willy's Livery across the street and tried the door. The stable was locked up for the night and there was no answer when he pounded on the side door. He wondered about breaking in to check the horses, then decided against it.

Instead, he crossed the street to the saloon.

A few lights were still burning inside, and there were a few diehard drinkers getting ready to greet the dawn with bleary eyes and furred mouths.

A flurry of snow blew down the street as Jubal went through the batwings. Inside, the air was blue with smoke and heavy with the smell of drinking.

'What'll it be?' The solitary barkeep looked half asleep. 'Make it fast. I wanta close up.'

'Whiskey,' Jubal said, glancing round. 'The good kind.'

'Ain't got but one kind,' grunted the bartender, filling a shot glass.

There was no sign of either ten Eyck or Greenhaugh, so Jubal asked about them.

'Friend,' sighed the barkeep, 'I tend to folks drinkin', nuthin' more. I don't ask their names an' I don't look at their faces. I figger to stay healthy that way.'

He went back to washing glasses, ignoring Jubal.

The whiskey was sharp, with the bitter edge of homebrew, but it warmed Jubal some as he studied the interior of the saloon. It was small and dirty with no sign of a staircase or any rooms opening off. Wherever ten Eyck was holed up, it wasn't here. Jubal emptied his glass and decided to leave it for the night. He needed sleep and tomorrow was time enough to find the outlaws.

He went back into the street and hurried to the hotel. His room was warm, and the bed looked unusually tempting. He stripped off and climbed under the sheets. In seconds he was asleep.

The morning was hidden behind a white curtain of falling snow. The frozen dirt of the streets was obscured beneath a thickening blanket barely marked by the hoofprints of the few horses yet abroad. Outside the Albion, a porter was sweeping the boardwalk clear and along the road Jubal could see braziers lit against the growing cold. It was just after six. He shaved and dressed, then ate a hurried breakfast before shrugging into the loden coat and setting out for Willy's Livery. He took the Spencer with him.

The wind had gotten up in the early hours and was now blowing with relentless force from out of a gloomy yellow sky. Jubal hiked the coat's hood over his derby and let his chin sink down inside the fastenings. He had to squint to see into the blizzard, but was still grateful for the unexpected help. With snow like this falling, ten Eyck was unlikely to risk leaving town on horseback, and there was no train due out for another day.

Jubal made straight for the stable.

The poorer section of Cheyenne was deep in snow by the

time he reached the livery. No one bothered to sweep the sidewalks here, and what paths existed were trodden down by passers-by. Mostly, the streets were empty.

The Red Dog was opening up as he reached the narrow street and across the way a youngster dressed in a worn, blue greatcoat was shovelling snow clear of the stable doors. Jubal waded through a knee-high drift and shouted at the kid.

The boy set his shovel down and walked over. Jubal ducked inside the stable.

'Can I help you, mister?' The youngster was no more than sixteen.

'Yeah.' Jubal reached a dollar from inside his jacket. 'There's three men left horses with you. Big chestnut, a black and a skewball. They still here?'

The boy looked doubtful for a moment. The sight of the dollar changed his mind.

'Yeah,' he said. 'They paid me a week in advance. Said they'd come back if they was stayin' on. I reckon they'll come by today. It don't look like travellin' weather, an' their time's up.'

Jubal passed the dollar over. 'Listen. There's another five for you if you let me know when they get here. Will you do that?' The boy nodded enthusiastically. 'Good. I'll be waiting over in the saloon.'

'I'll let you know soon as they arrive. You want I should send them over?'

'No.' Jubal shook his head. 'You want to make that other five, you just tell me.'

'Sure thing.' The kid winked conspiratorially. 'I won't let on.'

Jubal went back into the snow. There was no sign of it easing up and even the drab frontage of the Red Dog looked welcoming as a refuge from the cold.

The same barkeep he had seen the night before was piling logs into a pot-belly stove as Jubal went inside. If he recognized Jubal, he gave no sign. Just slammed the stove door shut and wiped his hands on an apron already dirty. He adjusted the vent to get a draught going inside the pot-belly and then ambled around the corner of the bar.

'What'll it be?'

'Whiskey,' said Jubal. 'I don't suppose you got any coffee.'

'You suppose right,' grunted the barkeep. 'I run a . . .'

'Saloon,' Jubal finished for him. 'Give me a shot and a beer.'

The bottle came off a dusty shelf behind the counter. It had no label and the contents tasted as bad as the night before. At least they took the chill off. The beer was better, even though Jubal would have preferred coffee: no great drinker, he was relatively unused to liquor this early in the day. He dropped some coins on the bar and carried his mug over to the window. It was dusty on the inside and frosted on the outside. Jubal used the sleeve of his coat to wipe a patch of grime clean, then decided he wouldn't see much anyway and hauled a chair round to face the door.

The barkeep was sweeping the floor before Jubal got settled down.

Jubal nursed the beer. No one else came in. The bartender finished sweeping and began to rearrange glasses along the counter. The snow got heavier. Jubal tugged the watch clear of his vest and flicked the cover open. It was seven and thirty minutes.

He ordered a second beer. It was served with the same sullen silence as before.

By ten, he had drunk four mugs and didn't want any more. He called for whiskey.

Around eleven, a few more people drifted in. They mostly took one fast drink and then hurried back to whatever work they had left for the quick warm-up. The barkeep leant on the counter, idly turning the pages of a newspaper.

Jubal drank another whiskey and watched the snow piling up in the street.

It was noon when the boy came hurrying through the door. He glanced round and spotted Jubal. His face was reddened by the wind, and his woolly cap was powdered white. He came over to Jubal's table and leaned down to whisper cautiously.

'There's one of them just come by. He give me the money fer another week an' said he wanted to check his horse over. He's in there now.'

'Only one?' Jubal stood up. 'What's he look like?'

'Tall, skinny feller.' The youngster was excited by the drama. 'He looked kinda worried. Got a black beard, an' when he shook the snow off his hat I saw he was partway bald.'

'Greenhaugh,' Jubal muttered. 'Thanks, kid.'

He got a five-dollar piece out and handed it to the boy.

'You look cold. Why not stay here and buy yourself a drink?'

The kid looked at Jubal, then down at the Spencer. He changed his mind about refusing.

'All right, mister. Whatever you say.'

Jubal stepped out on to the sidewalk. The wind was howling now, and the far side of the street was barely visible. He levered the rifle's action, then eased the hammer down before crossing over to the livery. When he reached the doorway cut into the main gates he pushed the hood back from his head and kicked the door open.

The stable was dark, the only light filtering dimly through the windows cut into the upper part of the rear and forward walls. Halfway down, a man in a dark coat was bent over the rear hoof of a skewball pony.

He looked up as the door swung shut behind Jubal.

'Kid?' It was Greenhaugh's voice. 'You got a forge attached? This shoe needs fixin'.'

Jubal moved forwards through the gloom. His boots made a dry, rustling sound on the fresh straw.

'You don't need a smithy,' he said coldly. 'You're not going anywhere.'

Greenhaugh failed to recognize Jubal's voice. He stood up, coming out of the stall.

'I want yore goddam advice, I'll ask fer it. I want this pony ready to go soon as this snow eases up.'

'Why?' Jubal moved closer. 'You got another robbery planned?'

'What? Who the hell are you?' Greenhaugh began to sound nervous. 'Step into the light.'

His hand fumbled at the buttons of his heavy coat. He got two open and was reaching in to his gun when Jubal came out of the shadows. He was holding the Spencer at hip height, the muzzle levelled on Greenhaugh's belly. The hammer made a sharp *click* as he snapped it back.

'Cade! Fer Chrissakes! Jubal Cade.'

'Hallo, Jeb.' Jubal's voice was flat, menacing. 'Where's Jacob?'

Greenhaugh dragged the pistol into view. It was a Colt's Frontier model, the long-barrelled kind. The foresight snagged on the lining of the coat and Greenhaugh mumbled a curse.

Jubal rammed the Spencer hard into the outlaw's stomach.

'Drop it, Jeb. Toss it into the hay.'

'Oh, Jesus!' Greenhaugh obeyed. 'How'd you find us?'

'I told you I'd come after you.' Jubal stared at the man, his brown eyes cold. 'Jimmy Schwatz was right back there on the river. You should have killed me.'

Greenhaugh was a tall man. He stood several inches above Jubal, but now he seemed shrunk in, hollowed by fear. He blinked, licking his lips. Sweat formed on his brow. Slowly, realization dawned on him.

'Jimmy,' he groaned. 'We heard he was shot. That was you.'

Jubal nodded. 'That's right, Jeb. I killed him. Now I want Jacob.'

Greenhaugh shook his head. His lips moved under his moustache and his hands fidgeted with his coat. He looked down at the rifle, then at Jubal's face. He swallowed.

'I can't. Jacob'd kill me.'

'I'll kill you,' remarked Jubal, almost conversationally. 'Where is he?'

Greenhaugh moaned and rubbed a hand across his beard. His shoulders began to tremble. Abruptly, he fell to his knees, mumbling incoherently. His head drooped and he braced both hands on the floor. Jubal stepped back a pace, still holding the rifle on the shuddering outlaw.

'You kill me an' you'll never find Jacob,' groaned the man.

'I can wait for him,' said Jubal. 'He'll come for his horse.'

'No.' Greenhaugh shook his head. 'If I don't show up, he'll know sumthin's wrong.'

'I can hurt you, Jeb.' Jubal's voice was calm, indifferent. 'I can make you tell.'

Greenhaugh gulped. He nodded slowly, then reached his right hand up to grasp the gatepost of the stall. 'All right.' He shifted his weight, preparatory to standing. His left side was turned away from Jubal, his arm hanging loose by his knees. Slowly, he began to rise.

He was halfway to his feet when he swung round, his left arm flashing out in a short, sweeping curve. Something spun loose from his hand and Jubal ducked instinctively.

The horseshoe Greenhaugh had picked up from the stall hit Jubal along the right side of his neck. He felt a numbing blow strike the nerve clusters between shoulder and jaw, and his right arm jerked with reflex action. His elbow was tugged up, so that the Spencer angled downwards as he squeezed the trigger. Greenhaugh went on turning, throwing himself sideways so that Jubal's bullet ploughed air above his legs.

Jubal turned, setting his back to the stall as he levered a fresh load into the Spencer.

Greenhaugh tumbled across the aisle and grabbed a tangle of harness strung off the opposite stall. He lurched round, flailing the tackle in a wide arc. The outermost section of the leather hit the barrel of the Spencer as Jubal pulled the trigger back. It turned the muzzle just far enough that the shot scorched a hole through the wing of Greenhaugh's coat without harming the outlaw. Greenhaugh hefted the tackle back, tangling it around the Spencer, and slung the harness at Jubal's face.

Jubal lifted the rifle to block the throw. Then Greenhaugh was on him.

The outlaw was driven by desperation and fear. Jubal felt a fist hammer against the side of his head. A knee ram into his groin. He dropped the rifle, gasping as pain flooded upwards through his bowels and doubled him over.

He fell to the floor and rolled, avoiding Greenhaugh's feet.

The pounding ceased and there was the sound of footsteps moving fast down the stable. Jubal turned on to his belly and pushed up on his hands and knees. His gut hurt and the right side of his neck was still numb. Greenhaugh was down the far end, tugging on the rear door. Jubal dragged himself upright and stumbled after the balding killer.

He reached the man and grabbed his shoulder, swinging him round. Greenhaugh ducked, deflecting Jubal's fist off his right shoulder. He swung his own arms upwards so that Jubal's hands were knocked clear, lifting above his head. Greenhaugh stooped and rammed his skull into Jubal's face. Jubal twisted, taking the blow on cheek and shoulder. He staggered back.

Greenhaugh kicked him and broke away. He ran for the front door.

Jubal saw the broom the stableboy had been using leaning against the wall. He grabbed it and threw it like a spear. The heavy head dragged the thing down, dropping it between Greenhaugh's legs so that the outlaw got tangled up and fell on his face.

Jubal started after him.

Greenhaugh got back on his feet and grabbed the broom. He swung it round, forcing Jubal to duck. He stabbed the thing at Jubal's face, and the smaller man backed away as the stiff bristles threatened to pierce his eyeballs. Greenhaugh shoved the broom against his chest, pitching him backwards, and jumped for the ladder going up to the lofts.

Willy's Livery was built like most western stables, on the pattern of a high-roofed barn. Stalls ran down both sides with a flat, unwalled balcony built over the booths to store fodder. The lofts were some twenty feet above the floor and mostly filled up with bales of hay and sacks of grain. There was a single, thirty-foot ladder used to reach the upper levels, shifted from side to side as needed. Greenhaugh reached the top while Jubal was still picking himself up, and began to clamber over the stacked bales towards the forward window.

The piled hay blocked off any chance of Jubal using a gun. And, besides, he wanted Greenhaugh alive. He went up the ladder.

The outlaw was crawling over the hay when Jubal reached him. He kicked back, slamming a heel against Jubal's outthrust hand. Jubal winced and crawled after.

Greenhaugh tumbled into a cleared space, where the bales had been lifted down. Jubal went after him.

He got a grip on the outlaw's legs and dragged him over.

Greenhaugh screamed and Jubal felt a hand fasten on his collar. Then a sudden tug. Then open space under him.

There was a sensation like a bad dream. When the world opens up and the dreamer is falling through nothingness. Just falling.

Jubal hit something – he was too winded to say what – and rolled sideways. He staggered to his feet and saw Greenhaugh limping away from a pile of sacks. They were layered four up from the stable's floor, spreading out three wide from the bars of the nearest stall. Across the top three sacks there was a deep indentation where the two bodies had hit.

Greenhaugh reached the far wall, close to the door.

Instead of going through, he took a billhook down off the wall and turned back to face Jubal.

The hook was recently sharpened. The curved edge glittered as Greenhaugh hefted it in sweeping cuts before his chest.

'You was right,' snarled the outlaw. 'Jimmy was right. We shoulda killed you.'

He advanced down the aisle of the stable, hacking the billhook in ugly arcs.

Jubal backed off.

He was hurting where Greenhaugh had kicked him, and his right shoulder was still numb. His legs were shaky from the fall and his hands were empty. Greenhaugh was too close to risk opening the loden coat to reach the pistol holstered under his jacket.

Greenhaugh smiled and came on forwards.

Jubal hit the ladder and tottered round it. Greenhaugh ran in, swinging the hook. The blade cut shards of wood from the ladder. Jubal backed farther down the aisle.

He stumbled into a second obstruction and shifted to the side as something hit him across the shoulders.

A long pole fell to the ground beside him. He reached down to grab the stick: it was his only defence.

When he got it in his hands he saw that it was a two-tined pitchfork, the kind used for lifting hay into the stalls. He backed off some more, swinging the fork round like a lance. Greenhaugh halted his advance.

Jubal darted the pitchfork at the outlaw's face. Greenhaugh swung the billhook to deflect the blow. He reached up, trying to grasp the shaft and run in under the tines. Jubal moved back, dragging him off balance. Greenhaugh held his grip, yanking the pole downwards. At the same time he cut the billhook round at Jubal's legs.

Jubal turned, twisting the shaft out of Greenhaugh's hand. He swung the fork across, scratching cloth loose from the outlaw's coat. Greenhaugh went with the blow, rolling his body on to the prongs, so that his weight threatened to rip the shaft clear of Jubal's grip.

Jubal swung the thing over the floor, sweeping it clear of Greenhaugh as the man scythed the billhook backwards and forwards above his rolling body. One blow hit the shaft of the fork and smashed it sideways across Jubal's ribs. Jubal went back against a stall. Inside, a horse squealed in fright and slammed its hooves against the gate. Jubal was pitched forwards.

Greenhaugh came up on his feet.

Jubal stepped back, twisting round and trying to regain his balance as he skidded over a patch of dung-fouled straw.

Greenhaugh arced the billhook at his stomach. Jubal went back. And felt his feet go out from under him.

He hit the floor and gasped as the force of the fall emptied his lungs. Greenhaugh laughed and sprang forwards with the hook lifting up over his head. His mouth was wide open and his eyes were staring in feral joy as he brought the heavy blade down in a killing stroke.

Jubal powered to the side. At the same time he swung the pitchfork up and over to line the prongs on Greenhaugh's face. The force of the outlaw's downswing prevented him from shifting out of line. The billhook sank inches deep into the floor. The right-hand tine of the fork went into his gaping mouth. It punctured his cheek and emerged at the back, just under his right ear, the blood-stained point sticking out between his jaws.

Greenhaugh screamed. Blood ran down his neck and chin. Jubal twisted the pitchfork, turning him off balance. Greenhaugh dropped the hook and tried to tug the pitchfork from his mouth. Jubal put his weight behind the pole and drove the man back across the stable as he climbed to his feet. Greenhaugh's teeth made a rasping sound on the dirty metal.

Jubal shoved him back against the stalls on the far side.

Greenhaugh felt the woodwork hit his back and squinted down the shaft of the pitchfork. He had both hands wrapped around the pole, but Jubal's weight held it firmly in place, the tine grating on teeth and jawbone.

'Where's Jacob?' It was a raw, ugly snarl. 'You ready to tell me?'

Greenhaugh tried to say *yes*. It came out as a gargle of blood.

Jubal yanked the fork back, ripping an inch-wide hole through the outlaw's cheek. He turned the fork as it cleared the face, thrusting down and forwards so that the curve of the prongs spanned Greenhaugh's neck, holding him pinned against the stall.

'Where is he?' Jubal rasped.

Tears ran down Jeb Greenhaugh's face. They mingled with the blood spilling from his cheek.

'There's a rooming house behind the Red Dog.' His voice was thick with blood and fear. 'He's in there with a girl. Her name's Lucy. Room's in her name.'

'He got the money with him?' Jubal grated. 'The money you took from the Kempton bank?'

Greenhaugh nodded as best he could with a pitchfork thrust against his neck.

'Yeah. Jacob kept it all. Said we shouldn't oughta spend it yet.'

'Good,' rasped Jubal. And eased the pitchfork clear.

Greenhaugh pressed a hand against his cheek. Blood ran from between his fingers, and when he spoke again his voice was throaty with terror.

'You gonna turn me in?'

'No.' Jubal shook his head. 'No point. It'd take too long to get word to Montana and back. I don't have that much time.'

Greenhaugh let a long, slow sigh whistle out between his teeth. Part of it came from the hole in his cheek. He was hurting, but it wasn't anything that wouldn't heal, given some time and a little care. The main thing was that he still lived. That was better than Jimmy Schwatz got. But he never had liked Jimmy much. Jumped-up little bastard with a quick mouth and an over-eager trigger finger. Hell! It was a good thing Jeb had helped the doc out back in Hope. And again along the river. He'd spoken up both times, hadn't he? Jimmy had wanted to kill the doc. Jeb hadn't. That was probably why Jubal was letting him go now. Shit! Jacob could take his chances. That was his worry, not Jeb's.

He looked at Jubal. Then at the pitchfork that was still pointed at his belly.

'You gonna let me go now, doc?'

'No,' Jubal said evenly. 'You owe too much. Those people back in Kempton and the others in Hope, they wouldn't like it.'

He rammed the pitchfork into Greenhaugh's belly as he spoke. The prongs sank deep through the coat and the shirt and the skin behind. They went through the wall of muscle guarding the stomach and pierced the inner sac. The right-hand tine lanced the heart, puncturing the right ventricle and grating on the spine behind. Jeb Greenhaugh's eyes opened very wide and a great pain filled his body to such an extent that all he could do was gasp in shock. The pitchfork tucked into his gut and the prongs burst out of his back. They sank into the woodwork of the stall, pinning him upright.

He opened his mouth and tried to say something, but a great swirling numbness filled up his mind and all he could do was hang there staring at Jubal.

'I couldn't let you go,' murmured the small man with the cold brown eyes. 'You get my point?'

CHAPTER FIFTEEN

Jacob ten Eyck woke up with a hangover.

There was a buzzing inside his skull and his mouth tasted like the sole of a goat's slipper. When he opened his eyes it felt like a flare had gone off and burned his brain. He groaned and eased the sheets over his head. They stank of whiskey and sweat and sex. He pushed them away again and sat up. For a moment he wondered who owned the body snoring beside him. Then he remembered: Lucy. Lucy Jourdan. He'd promised her a trip to Paris on the strength of the Kempton take. Paris, France. In a white carriage, for Chrissakes.

He looked at the dark spill of hair covering the other pillow. Saw the shading of white at the roots. And wondered what had made him say that.

Christ! It wasn't the first time he'd made a whore a promise. Nor the first time he'd broken one.

Lucy wasn't bad. In bed she was goddam good. But she wasn't exactly the kind of lady a man with money liked to be seen with.

And Jacob was sitting right on top of nearly twenty-seven thousand dollars.

Take off the few hundred spent buying railroad tickets and horses, maybe a hundred more for expenses around Cheyenne. That still left at least twenty-six thousand in clean, negotiable notes.

It was a lot of money.

Enough to buy a man a good time. Even a ranch and a decent herd – if that was what the man wanted. In Jacob's case it wasn't. He knew nothing at all about ranching, other than that brief experience of punching cows. And all that had done was convince him he didn't like it.

No. He needed spending money. Money that could be used. Invested. Money in a bank gathered interest. Money bought land, or houses. In the East. There were things like shares and stocks. He didn't understand them, but he knew they kept a man going. It would take some kind of fancy-suited accountant to tell him how, but with that kind of money he could live high on the hog. Even after the money man creamed off his cut. But that was fair enough, it would still leave Jacob a tidy sum. And if the man in the suit argued, he could be shot.

Jimmy and Jeb were the problem.

They'd expect equal thirds of the take. Even though it had been his idea to hit Kempton from the start.

That would cut his share down to nine thousand.

Not enough to cut clear of all the states and the territories that had dodgers with his face on them and rewards for anyone who killed him.

The whole sum was better. Leave Jimmy and Jeb to look after themselves. Take the whole bag of money. All twenty-six thousand of it. Christ! Pieter was dead now so there was nothing to do for the family. Jimmy and Jeb weren't much use any more. Gunhands was all they'd ever been. Leave them. That was the sensible move. Leave them and the blowsy lump in the bed. Paris? Shit! She'd end in a stinking Tularosa alley.

But Jacob ten Eyck would be living high. Living off the hog.

Just as soon as he got loose of Schwatz and Greenhaugh.

He scratched his chest while he thought about it. If the rumours he'd heard were right, Jimmy was no longer a problem. Most likely, the touchy little bastard had got into a whore-house fight and lost. Jacob hoped so: it made his problem that much easier.

Jeb, now, he was a simpler proposition. He was scared of Jacob; probably too scared to risk a straight-up fight. But he was sneaky, and with that much money at stake he might find the spirit he usually lacked. Jacob didn't doubt but that he could take Jeb in a fight, but that could lead to awkward questions from the law. If this damn' snow hadn't closed Cheyenne down tighter than a nun's legs he could take Jeb out on to the prairie and leave him there for the buzzards and the coyotes. But now a horse couldn't make a short mile out of town.

Jacob scratched some more and reached for the bottle beside the bed. He drank from the neck, shuddering as the dog stood up and bristled its hair. Then he got it.

There was a train due out today or tomorrow. He could buy tickets through to St Louis. That should leave Jeb stranded. Even if he had the money to follow on, it would be days before another train fought through the snow. And by then Jacob could be down the river to New Orleans or holed up in a city too big for one man to winkle him out.

Jacob congratulated himself and swung his legs clear of the bed.

Lucy Jourdan woke up at the movement and opened bleary eyes.

'Where you goin', honey?'

Christ! She looked ugly of a sudden. Jacob wondered how she'd managed to look so good before. It just showed what Winter and going without could do to a man. But she might still be useful. To put Jeb off the scent, if for nothing else.

'Down to the KP depot. No reason to wait on here when we could be headed East. I'm gonna buy us tickets to St Louis. After that, it's Paris, France, an' a high ole time.'

Lucy smiled and reached a hand across to fondle his chest.

'You're real good to me, Jacob. I appreciate that.' She ran a tongue over her lips. 'I'll show you how much.'

'Not now,' said ten Eyck. 'I wanta buy those tickets. You just stay snug, an' if anyone comes askin' fer me, you tell 'em I went to get a new gun.'

'Jeb, too?' She sat up, exposing heavy breasts marked with small bites.

Shit! They looked bad. Sagged down with too much flesh. Damn' near wrinkled now that he looked closer.

'Sure,' smiled Jacob, 'Jeb, too. This is our secret. It's just you an' me.'

He pulled on his coat and tucked a Colt's Peacemaker into the right-hand pocket. The barrel was cut down to about three inches. It was his hideaway gun, easier to use than the full-size pistol holstered under the stormproof. Then he went out of the room and struggled through the snow towards the depot.

Lucy Jourdan eased back against the pillows, letting her mind wander over the prospect of St Louis and New Orleans and Paris. She didn't particularly want to go to Paris because it was foreign, and she didn't like foreigners much. Jacob was Dutch, sure, but that was different. He had money and he was taking her away from Cheyenne. It was a working girl's dream: a man with money who wanted her to spend it on. So, if Paris was where he was headed, she'd follow on. She spoke some of the language, at least. *Madame. Sillvoo play. Soixante neuf. Mercy. Vooly voo dur oo traw dang la chambraw. Missoor.* Whoring round the cow towns didn't just let a girl build up a stake; it gave her an education, too.

She had nearly two hundred dollars tucked away in the bank. Maybe she'd draw the account before they left. Just before. And without telling Jacob. He had enough of his own money already. And a girl needed an insurance policy. She climbed out of bed and went over to the washstand. Splashing water on her face and under her arms, she began to hum softly. She wanted to look nice for Jacob when he got back. He deserved that.

She damped her hair and combed it through. The make-up would last another day before it needed replenishing. Except for the lipstick, which she coated red across her mouth.

She wondered about the dampness between her legs. It might be best if she washed that a bit. She pulled the plug on the bowl and then filled the pan with fresh water. Setting it down on the dirty carpet, she squatted and began to splash water between her thighs.

Then the door opened.

And a man came in with a rifle stuck out in front of him like the first weapon she had ever seen. She jumped up, squealing.

'You bastard! You made me piss. Fuck off!'

'Where's Jacob?' said Jubal Cade.

Lucy stepped back from the bowl. She made no attempt to hide her nakedness. Rather, she flaunted it.

'He ain't here. You can search, if you want. He went to buy a gun.'

Jubal glanced round the room. The bed was rumpled and stained, like the naked woman glaring at him from across the tattered carpet. There was a narrow cupboard, too small for a man to hide in, and the bed was high enough off the floor that he could see the whiskey bottle and the emptiness beneath.

He paced over to the woman and levelled the Spencer on her belly.

'Where'd he go? Schwatz and Greenhaugh are dead. Jacob's not coming back for you.'

'He will.' Her voice was filled with too much certainty for Jubal to doubt it. 'He has to.'

'Why?'

She shook her head. Jubal dropped the muzzle of the Spencer so that it nestled against the dark brush of her pubic hairs. He thrust the rifle forwards and down. Lucy Jourdan gasped and lifted up.

'I could give you the biggest bang of your life,' said Jubal. 'And then wait for Jacob. Except he won't be coming back. Maybe I should do that. It doesn't matter to me.'

Lucy tried to walk clear of the barrel. Jubal paced her over the carpet until she hit the wall behind and froze. He lifted the Spencer, running the muzzle upwards through her hair. He traced a line that ended at her navel, then drifted the gun down again to centre on the cleft of her legs.

'Why does he have to come back?' His voice was flat and cold and angry. 'Tell me.'

Lucy Jourdan thought about Paris and white carriages and money. Then she looked at the man in the bloodstained coat and down at the rifle. And made a choice.

'His money's here.' Hope emptied from her mind like the fear-spilled urine from her body. 'It's under the bed. Take it. For Chrissakes, take it! Get that away from me!'

'You didn't tell me where he went,' rasped Jubal. 'I have to know that, too.'

'The rail depot. He was goin' to buy tickets on the KP. To St Louis. For the two of us.'

Jubal eased the Spencer back from between her legs. Lucy sighed and slid down the wall. She felt her dreams fading away like smoke in the wind. Thank God she hadn't told Jacob about her bank account. She smiled tentatively.

'You gonna take it, mister? You gonna take all that money?'

'Sure,' said Jubal. 'It belongs to other people.'

'We could have a real good time with that,' Lucy simpered. 'Just you an' me.'

136

She let her legs spread out as Jubal tugged the sacks from under the bed. She smiled, touching her breasts so that the nipples stood up, and let her tongue drift over her lips.

'You an' me. We could be together. Take a train to St Louis an' live high. I could be real good to you.'

Jubal looked at her. She had let herself go for too long to be truly attractive, but the original design was still visible under the excess flesh. A man in urgent need might be tempted: there was an aura of succulent decadence about her. He felt suddenly guilty. Guilty for losing the memory of Mary, his wife. Guilty for forgetting why he was there, even though it was only for a moment. It had been a long time.

But he was still determined to carry his first deal through.

He shook his head and lifted the sacks on to his shoulder.

'You bastard! You goddam freakin' bastard!'

Lucy's voice followed him down the corridor.

It stayed with him as he went down the street and dumped the sacks of money in the marshal's office.

The deputy called Hank was there, manning the station while Bill Dupree made his morning rounds. Jubal piled the bags on the desk, ignoring the papers they crushed and the inkwell they spilled. He got Hank to sign a receipt that he folded into his jacket.

Then he waded through the snow to the depot of the Kansas-Pacific Railroad.

The tracks were deep under the snow, and from a long way down the line he heard the whistle of a shunting engine coming up with a plough mounted on the front to clear a path for the passenger train. The shunter was out from Denver, cutting a path for the delayed Baldwin scheduled to haul goods and passengers clear of Cheyenne. It was about a mile off, judging by the smoke drifting up from the white emptiness south of the depot.

He went to the ticket office to ask about travellers.

Yes, there had been a tall, bearded man bought tickets through to St Louis. A big man in a dark green storm-coat. He was in the saloon across the way, waiting for news of clearance.

The saloon was a dingy place called the Snow Queen.

Jubal went in.

Jacob ten Eyck was sitting at a table close to the door. He failed to recognize Jubal until the Spencer slammed down on the table, tumbling glasses and a half-drunk bottle to the saw-dusted floor.

Ten Eyck kept his hands in view and grinned at the cocked rifle.

'You found me.'

It was statement, not question. Jubal nodded.

'What you gonna do? Take me in? You can't prove a damn' thing.'

'No, I can't.' Jubal smiled. It was a cold, ugly smile. 'But I got the money. I left it with the marshal's office.'

Jacob looked worried. 'You killed Jimmy?'

'And Jeb,' rasped Jubal. 'Like you say, I can't prove a thing here. That's why I have to take you back to Kempton. Or kill you.'

'In front of all these witnesses?' grinned ten Eyck. 'You shoot me here an' you're branded killer. You try to take me back an' I'll jump you along the way. It ain't worth it, Cade.'

Jubal shrugged. 'Matter of opinion. I figure I owe it. There was a man back in Kempton hired me to bring you in. You, or the money. I got the money from your whore. Taking you is something I owe to Charity Lambert and all those other people you killed.'

He stepped back from the table and hefted the Spencer upwards.

'Stand up, Jacob. It's time you paid your debts.'

'I'll decide that,' snarled ten Eyck.

And fired the hideaway gun.

The bullet ripped a hole through the pocket of his coat. The cloth slowed its passage a bit, and it struck the rim of the table as it blasted at Jubal's face. Jubal sensed the movement and powered backwards as ten Eyck raised his hand. The bullet clipped his cheek. The Spencer went off with a sudden thunder of sound as Jacob spilled sideways from his chair. He kicked the table over against Jubal's legs and went out through the window in a shower of broken glass.

Jubal fell down. Twisted over on to his belly and writhed out under the batwings with the Spencer lifting to sight on the street.

The doors flew back as two shots splintered chips from the woodwork.

Then ten Eyck was up and running for the rail depot.

Jubal went through the snow after him.

Jacob got in amongst the buildings and began to work his way down towards the oncoming train. He opened his coat so that he could draw the Frontier Colt holstered on his belt. He crouched behind a stack of timber, waiting for Jubal to show.

Jubal came over at a run. There was a thin spill of blood marking ten Eyck's passage, and he followed it through the outbuildings of the depot. He came around a corner where a storehouse and a station building formed a narrow alley, and paused.

Jacob was carrying two guns, both faster to fire than the Spencer. But the rifle had the greater range. The winning had to depend on who took the best position. Jubal looked round. The buildings ran on ahead into the tangle of the stockyards. There was wood piled up in twenty-foot stacks between the shacks and the yards. Jacob could be anywhere.

Across from his position, the rails opened out on to the emptiness of the snow-covered prairie.

Down the line, the shunt-engine howled a lonesome cry.

Jubal ducked round the side of the nearest building. A shot blasted from the woodpile up the way. He twisted, putting the shack's wall between himself and Jacob ten Eyck's guns.

The shack was some kind of storage place. It spanned the whole length of the alley between the tracks and the outer street. It was low and roofed shallow, almost flat. Jubal stepped up on to the porch and shoved the Spencer upwards over the snow-covered shingles. He grabbed the gutter and hauled himself after the rifle, butting the gun with his head to stop it sliding off. It was hard going, clambering up over the snow, but he made it to the apex of the low roof and looked down across the yards.

Jacob ten Eyck was crouched down behind a tall stack of wood, only his arm visible as he waited for Jubal to come round the corner of the sheds.

Jubal fired twice from the top of the building, sending Jacob back under cover.

Then he swung his legs over the angle of the roof and went down the far side like a child skinny-sliding a toboggan run. He came off the edge in a skirl of falling snow and hit the drifts beneath. Snow cushioned his fall, and he rolled, twisting to the left where spilled logs had tumbled from the main stack.

He came up on his feet and powered on to the logs. Timber shifted under his feet, rolling down as he danced his way to the top. There was a shot, and he dropped flat, angling the Spencer down and firing blind. He rolled sideways, feeling the logs move under him.

There was a thick rope close by his face, holding the main bundle of timber in place. To his left, closest to the tracks, the rope had rotted away. To his right the third line was frayed. The bulk of the logs was held by the central cord.

Jacob ran out from the far side and fired two-handed at Jubal.

Shards of wood splintered upwards.

Jubal ducked back and pressed the muzzle of the Spencer to the central rope. He fired. Fired again as ten Eyck triggered blind shots into the timber.

The rope parted, and Jubal lifted upright, leaping clear as the whole stack moved and began to roll out from under him.

He landed in a drift, powering sideways as the logs tumbled into the alleyways to either side. He caught a brief glimpse of ten Eyck as the outlaw turned and ran from the path of the falling logs. Snow obscured his vision, thrown up by the spill of timber, and he huddled into the drift, hoping none would land across him.

When he looked up, ten Eyck was running down the rails and logs were bouncing all over.

The outlaw had a gun in both hands, but he was mainly concerned with fighting clear of the threat from the logs. Jubal lifted up on one knee and sighted down the barrel of the Spencer. He flicked snow clear from the foresight and blew a thick cluster loose of the vee-notched rearsight.

Then he fired.

The .30 calibre slug hit Jacob ten Eyck at a range of around one hundred and fifty feet. It punched through his coat and went in beneath his left shoulderblade. His clavicle shattered, twisting his left arm up and out so that the short-barrelled Colt flew loose from suddenly nerveless fingers and he spun round under the impact. That presented the right side of his body to Jubal's second shot. The bullet hit as Jacob lifted the other Colt to fire back. It went in through his ribs and ricocheted off the curve of bone to nick his spine. He jerked upright, screaming as he twisted, and fell down into the path of the third shot. It hit his sternum, glancing off the heavy bone so that it deflected upwards and tore out through his upper chest into his jaw. Slowed by the passage through cloth and flesh and bone, the bullet lodged in his jaw, breaking it and splintering teeth.

Jacob ten Eyck fell down on the snow and spat blood and broken teeth and half his tongue. He still held the Colt. He even tried to lift it again to fire at Jubal.

The shunt-engine yowled a warning and Jubal smiled a cold and empty grin as he lowered the Spencer.

Ten Eyck heard the sound and dropped his gun. He pushed his bleeding body over and looked up into the grid of the snow-plough mounted ahead of the engine.

He raised his arms, screaming as the bulk of the heavy metal thundered towards him. His hands touched the plough. Then his arms broke under the weight and the tip caught his body. The weight of snow behind him acted as a barrier, driving him down and on to the main grid of the plough. His ribs collapsed, then his legs curled up and got caught in the metal. There was a thick spurt of bright crimson, like a fountain against the white. And Jacob ten Eyck disappeared under the snow and the train.

The locomotive stopped in a screeching halt alongside Jubal's position. There was a wide swath of red-speckled snow strung out behind it. At the front, a bloodstained hand stuck up like a marker post. Blood dripped from the raw fingers.

The stoker climbed down from the cab and emptied his stomach over the remains of Jacob ten Eyck. The driver followed him, then turned to Jubal.

'What in the hell happened? Why'd that madman come out like that?'

Jubal shrugged. 'Don't worry about it. He was just a feller who went off the rails.'

Marshal Dupree wanted to know why Jubal had been chasing Jacob and the others.

He wanted to know why a stablehand could identify Jubal as the man who had paid him to quit the stable just before a body was found pinned on a fork. And why Jubal was shooting at a man who ran under a train.

Now that it was all done, Jubal decided to explain. He told Dupree about Kempton and Hope, and all the other killings attributed to the ten Eyck gang. Dupree checked through his posters and came up with five that bore resemblance to Jacob's pack. Two looked like Jimmy Schwatz, but he couldn't be identified any more. One was like Jeb Greenhaugh. It carried a five hundred dollar reward in Nebraska. The other two showed faces that looked just like Jacob and Pieter ten Eyck. There was a thousand dollars offered on them, for the capture – dead or alive – of the Dutchman's Gang.

Jubal had never known that they were called that, but he took the money just the same. There didn't seem much reason why he shouldn't. He also took a paper from Dupree to establish that he had 'apprehended' the gang, and a second from the bank to establish that the bulk of Hodge's money would be transferred to Montana through official channels. He bought himself a through ticket on the next train north. It would take time to make the overland journey to Kempton, but Hodge still owed him the balance of the reward.

Marshal Dupree came down to the depot to see him on to the train.

'Stay outta trouble,' warned the lawman.

'I'll try,' Jubal nodded, 'but it seems to follow me around. Like that legend.'

'What legend?' Dupree looked confused.

Jubal grinned. 'You must have heard it. The one about the dying Dutchman.'